CASSIE MINT

Grumps Unleashed
The Complete Series

BLACK CHERRY
PUBLISHING

Contents

I

Grump Gone Wild

Description

⁙

I 'm fake-dating the man of my dreams.

But these feelings? They're all too real.

Here's some friendly advice, from me to you: don't ever fall for your grumpy boss.

And here's another top tip: when said boss asks you to fake-date in front of his awful snooty family, say no. Run fast and run far.

Whatever you do, don't mix up what's real and what's fake. Don't fall for his hungry stares, don't let your touches linger, and *definitely* don't sneak off into a hedge maze together. What good could come of it?

Remember: it's all a lie. A perfect, delicious, *tingly* lie.

And he's just playing a role.

Isn't he?

Fliss

My boss pops the question on a rainy Thursday after lunch.

Not *the* question, obviously. That would be too perfect, too dreamlike—and pretty weird, since for all the years I've worked for him, despite my ginormous crush, Sebastian Bamford has only ever seen me as his zany assistant.

No, the beautiful genius summons me into his top floor office with a few curt words through the intercom, then waits behind his huge desk, jaw clenched.

"Felicity."

Despite my nudging, he's only ever called me Fliss twice in our whole acquaintance. Once at the company holiday party two years ago, when he greeted me solemnly by the pop up bar. I remember it vividly, not just because of the name thing, but because he wore a black knitted sweater instead of his usual suit, and his cheeks were pink from walking down the frosty street. *Swoon.*

The second time was when I had three days off work with a

5

stomach flu. Sebastian called me at home on the third day, to 'check whether I needed anything'. Really, I think he suspected I was playing hooky.

Um, as if.

Not because I care so much about emails and appointments and refilling the water cooler cups, to be clear. But to willingly lose a day with Sebastian Bamford? The sexy, bossy nerd of my dreams? Are you crazy?

"I have a strange request." He's staring out of the huge windows. Raindrops patter against the glass, then streak down and blur the city skyline. Downtown looks like one giant smudge.

"Okay. What is it, sir?"

His mouth flattens, and he keeps scowling outside. I wait, shifting from foot to foot, but... nothing.

Alrighty.

I'm used to my boss's moods, so I distract myself with mental notes. Like: that potted plant in the corner needs water. And Sebastian has that video conference at two, the one with the German team. Should I double-check the translator? Wait, I did that already. But should I triple-check?

"It's not work-related," he says.

I bite the inside of my cheek, suddenly laser-focused. The air hums through the AC. "I'm very discreet, sir. You can trust me."

Trust me... Confide in me... Maybe love me back one day...

Are you listening, universe? Just putting it out there.

"It's delicate," Sebastian says.

He's killing me here. "I'm sure I can handle it."

Because seriously, whatever it is, I've got this. Picking up his dry cleaning? Booking a doctor's appointment? Lying to

6

his awful family for him? I'm there, no sweat, because I've been gone for my boss since day one. G-O-N-E. Head over heels for this beautiful grump, with his neat bronze hair and his tortoiseshell glasses and his perfectly pressed suits. I love him so much, it gives me indigestion.

When he rumbles orders at me in that deep voice—it's like he's reading me a sonnet. When he ignores me in the elevator, I swoon.

Gray eyes find mine, and shivers race down my spine. My face heats, despite the cool air flowing through a vent on the wall. This building should have a warning right above the entrance—*Caution: Boss may cause dizziness.*

"I have no right to ask you this, Felicity." He's so solemn; so pained. The rain-dulled daylight barely reaches his desk, and he's lit by the golden glow of a table lamp. "If you say no, it won't affect your work at all. Is that understood?"

Color me intrigued… though for the record, I'd do virtually anything for this man, including commit petty crimes. For Sebastian Bamford, my morals are scanty as hell.

He's just so *noble*. And hardworking and stern and delicious. Every second I'm near him, my fingers itch to yank on his tie. I want to climb into his lap and kiss him so hard I knock his glasses askew.

"Understood. What is it, sir?"

A muscle leaps in his jaw. Sebastian frowns over my shoulder into space, and the lamplight glints against his bronze hair. "I have a family event next weekend," he says slowly. "An important one, and… I need a date."

Oh my god. Oh my god.

Eeee!

I'm beaming wide, already floating up near the ceiling when

he adds: "I'd like you to pretend to be my girlfriend. It would be fake, obviously. You'd get overtime."

I crash back down to the floor.

Overtime? He wants to pay me for this?

...Fake?

"It's purely business," Sebastian says, still frowning over my shoulder. When he finally looks at me, concern darts through his gray eyes. Guess my dismay is splashed all over my face. "I can hire someone else," he adds quickly. "I don't want to make you uncomfortable, Felicity. But I have neither the time nor the inclination to find a real date, and... well, you know my family."

After our four years together, I certainly do. They're a pack of designer-suited jackals.

Whenever my grouchy sweetheart of a boss goes down the coast for family events, he always comes back looking worn down by life and five years older. At this rate, he'll be a crumbly old man before I've hit thirty, and who wants that?

"I'll do it," I say. Never mind my bruised heart; I will rescue this buttoned-down grump from his nefarious relatives. "But I'm... you know..."

I wave a hand up and down my body. My boss's mouth twists, and his gaze rakes me from head to toe, cataloging my many flaws.

The crinkly, too-bright clothes, covered with a fine layer of cat hair; the bruise on my knee from roller derby. My messy hair that always escapes from whatever bun or braid I put it in. Take your pick.

Is he gonna change his mind? My fingers pluck at my purple skirt, and I swallow hard. Maybe he'll take it back and ask someone more suitable. Because let's be honest: if Sebastian wants to impress his snooty family, I'm the last girl in the world he should choose.

"No," Sebastian declares, stern eyes fixed on an ink stain on my cuff. "I need it to be you, Felicity. I'll coach you."

Oh, great. Learning all the ways I don't measure up for this man? Sounds like pure torture.

Because the Bamfords are old money. Country clubs and race horses and private vineyards—*that* kind of money. And I have raspberry streaks in my hair and a tattoo of my ancient cat Rusty on my wrist. My bus pass has seen more action than my credit card.

"Awesome," I say.

But as I slink out of his office, my bruised heart dragging along the carpet, I try to see the positive side.

And that is: a weekend event with my boss. Hours and hours together away from the office. A sneak peek at his origins, and the chance to give the evil eye to his awful relatives. Sounds fun.

And who knows? Maybe pretending to date me will open Sebastian's eyes! Maybe he'll scoop me over his shoulder like a bespectacled Tarzan and carry me into the sunset.

Yeah, right. Girls like me don't land dreamboats like this. We nurse our forbidden crushes, then go home alone and snuggle with our stinky old cats.

Hope Rusty is ready to be the little spoon when I get home. Today's been a doozy.

Sebastian

"**S**tand up straight. Okay, try smiling for me." Hmm. "Can you show fewer teeth?"

A week later, I'm in the penthouse office with Felicity and a personal stylist after hours. The sky is navy blue outside, the city skyline hazy with electric light. Stars glitter high above as I coach my assistant in the Bamford ways, the stylist tutting and fussing.

We could be here for a while.

Felicity huffs and pushes her shoulders back. The bland smile she pastes on looks so fake it's painful.

…Or maybe this won't take long at all. "That's spot on. Well done."

Circling her slowly, I examine the outfit I ordered. Dressed in an austere cream dress with her hair pinned up to hide the pink streaks, Felicity looks… normal. Not at all like the human hurricane I'm used to.

My chest pinches, but I ignore it.

You know… this dress fits her well. Perhaps *too* well. "Is this appropriate?" I ask Pamela the stylist, waving a hand down my assistant's body, lingering where the cream fabric nips in at her slender waist then flares out with her hips. The sight makes my throat catch.

Pamela hums and taps her chin with a lacquered nail. In her early fifties, with coiffed blonde hair and pink lipstick, this woman has observed the Bamford set for decades. She knows our ways. "We'll have to hide the tattoo."

I cross to the desk where we laid out the accessories ready. There are diamond bracelets, drop earrings, and a pearl-studded watch. Silk scarves and a designer clutch.

"Rusty?" Felicity asks, her eyes going wide. She wraps one hand around her wrist, like she's protecting her cat from us villains. "What's wrong with him?"

Besides the tiny scratch he gave her thumb once? I still haven't forgiven the little flea bag for that, even if Felicity insists it was an accident.

"Nothing, except that the Bamfords think tattoos are for lower life forms." I nod at the desk. "Pick something to cover him up. Whatever you choose, you can keep."

That's fair, right? And not at all a roundabout way to give my assistant gifts.

Leaning against the desk, I wait as Felicity stomps over, wobbling in the heels I ordered. Her cheeks are flushed, and she scowls at the accessories. She won't meet my eye.

"*Lower life forms*," she mutters, prodding at the bracelets. "So gross."

"I don't think that," I hear myself say, as if my plucky assistant cares what her boring, repressed boss thinks of her appearance. Felicity Lovegood is pure sunshine, and no one could dim her glow.

Not even Pamela and I with our etiquette lessons. Not even the Bamfords. That's why I asked for this favor.

Felicity is snob-proof.

Case in point: "I would never wear any of these," she declares, waving at the priceless jewelry. "And if I did, I'd get mugged in two seconds flat."

She would? Is her area really that bad?

No, I don't like that. I don't like that at all.

The desk creaks as I lean back, my brain whirring. Could I pay for her to lodge closer to the office? Or nearer to my building, maybe? My driver could bring us both here in the mornings. Would she ever allow that?

"There's a make-up alternative," Pamela says, cutting through my daydream of Felicity piling into the backseat of my car each morning, fresh-faced and happy. Safe from mugging, her skirt riding up her thighs as she sits close to me, filling my lungs with her red berry scent. "But you'd have to be careful not to stain the dress."

They huddle together, strategizing. Outside, the wind lashes the skyscraper windows, dulled to a faint roar by the thick glass. In the distance, lightning spears through the night sky.

A minute later, Felicity is so solemn as she fixes the pearl-studded watch around her wrist. It covers most of Rusty, with only the tips of his ears poking out.

Though she usually never stops grinning, Felicity has barely smiled once since we met Pamela in here. In fact, she's been acting strangely all week, chatting less and avoiding my eyes. Her shoulders have been permanently slumped.

Does she regret agreeing to this? Well, who can blame her?

"Give us a moment please, Pamela."

The stylist's footsteps echo away down the hall, and I wait

12

until the water cooler gurgles far away by the elevator. Felicity fiddles with the watch, setting the time by the clock on the wall. Her dark hair is flawless.

I miss those pink streaks.

"I realize this may be unpleasant for you." With Pamela gone, I speak more softly, voice hushed. Though there's one less person in the room, my office suddenly feels smaller. More intimate. "But you can change your mind. As I said, it won't affect your work."

Felicity chews on her bottom lip, and when her eyes flick up to mine, I grip the edge of the desk harder.

God.

This is why I rarely stay late in the office. I'd rather finish my work at home, with a safe amount of distance between Felicity and I. Otherwise, the hush of the building and the darkened skies, the knowledge that we're alone... they get to me.

Not appropriate.

"It's fine," Felicity says. "No problemo. I can play dress up for a weekend—I did it all the time as a kid. I can pretend to be someone I'm not."

Pretend to be my girlfriend, in fact. I clear my throat, glancing at the doorway. Should I mention this? We're still alone.

"For my family to believe our ruse, I'll need to... touch you. Appear intimate with you." My pulse spikes at the mere thought.

Felicity snorts, though her smile seems bitter. "Think you can handle it, Mr B?"

Honestly? I'm not sure.

But it's not me I'm worried about. *I'm* the boss in this situation; I'm the one crossing a line. Who cares what I think?

"Perhaps we should rehearse that too. Set some boundaries." God knows I need them. "You can tell me what you're comfortable with, and I'll respect that, I promise. I won't take advantage."

"Too bad," Felicity murmurs, so quietly I nearly miss it. I blink, stunned—but she's teasing me, clearly. Always teasing.

My assistant steps closer, coming to stand within arm's length, and every thought leaves my brain except one: *Touch her. Touch her.*

Obviously, I ignore my caveman impulses. Like I said, I've had four years of practice, because whenever my assistant stands this close to me, all the nerves tingle under my skin. I breathe heavier, and it's like my senses are heightened. I hear every gust of wind outside; smell every ingredient in her fruity shampoo; feel the warmth radiating off her body.

Not. Appropriate.

"Okay," Felicity says. "Do your worst, sir. How are you gonna touch me in front of your folks?"

This is a bad idea. What was I thinking, suggesting this? It's a HR nightmare just waiting to happen. But my hand lifts, and I watch it like it belongs to someone else as it coasts along Felicity's slender shoulder, then slides down her tanned arm. Her skin is so warm and smooth, and my gut twists.

Our fingers knot together.

"Like this?" I rasp.

Her hazel eyes dart up to mine then away. "Okay, that's fine. What else?"

I should let go of her hand, but since she's squeezing me back, I don't want to. So I lift our joined hands instead, and slide my thumb over her pinned-up hair. It's so fussy in this style, so un-Felicity, and I'd love to pull it loose over her shoulders;

to grab a dark handful and press my face against it, breathing deep.

But that would be bad. And nothing I'd do in front of the Bamfords anyway, so what would be my excuse?

"Hm," I say when she peers up at me, lips parted. Her chest rises and falls a little faster too, the motion hypnotic beneath the cream dress, but I don't let myself look properly. "Now what? I'm open to suggestions."

Her eye roll is fond, thank god, and when Felicity spreads her free hand over my chest, my heartbeat lunges against her palm. Like it might burst through my shirt to reach her.

"Haven't you ever taken a girlfriend home before?"

My face heats. "No. That's why I need a fake date this time. My family keeps trying to set me up. They think I'm defective somehow."

"Because you don't parade your personal life in front of them?" Felicity scoffs, shaking her head, and her hand rubs a gentle circle on my chest. It's like she doesn't realize she's stroking me, too busy glaring up at me, so mad at the Bamfords.

On my behalf. How alien.

"Felicity," I grind out.

"Fliss," she says, tugging my tie straight like she's done it a thousand times before. "My fake boyfriends call me Fliss. Keep up, sir."

Sir.

Heat pounds through my veins, and I reach for her. There's no plan, no innocent touch I want to rehearse, just pure need to feel her skin beneath my palm.

"Cocktail dresses next," Pamela calls, her heels thudding down the corridor, and we spring apart just in time for her to waltz through the door. The stylist glances between us, but she doesn't mention our flushed cheeks or my guilty expression. "And you mentioned a garden party, Mr Bamford?"

"Ah. Yes."

Felicity gives a strained laugh. She raises both eyebrows at me. "This is going to be fun."

I don't think she means the garden party, somehow.

Staring out at the stars, I will my heartbeat to slow down.

Fliss

‿❧❦❧‿

The Bamford estate is on the coast, perched on the cliffs so the family can survey their kingdom. They have an ivy-clad mansion with columns and stone balconies; rolling grounds with water features and a hedge maze; gazebos and rose bushes and more.

Sebastian showed me pictures to prep me, but as we arrive on Friday evening, I still want to throw up.

Yeah. It's nothing like the shabby chic apartment I rent with two roommates, that's for sure. The security hut that opens the gates to the grounds is bigger than our living room.

"Snazzy." I watch the wrought iron gates swing open, our car idling beside the hut. My mouth is so dry. "Bet the school bus had fun dropping you off as a kid."

Sebastian hums, staring out of his own tinted window. He's not listening, lost in his own thoughts. It's been a long day already.

Lanterns glow in a winding snake through the grounds, following the half-mile path to the mansion, and string lights mingle with spring blossoms in the trees. Our car purrs along, the engine quiet.

Night's drawing in. Maybe I'll blend in better in low light? I adjust the pearl-studded watch on my wrist for the millionth time, trying to cover the tips of Rusty's ears.

My roommate Priya is taking care of him this weekend. I miss my little fur ball already.

"Brace yourself." Sebastian's low voice makes me jump, the sound so shocking after what feels like hours of tense silence. He's watching me closely, the pink sunset casting a warm glow on his face. "My family will want to test you, Felicity. Think of this as the world's worst job interview."

"Fliss," I say automatically, smoothing my dress over my lap. It's knee-length and blue, and I'm pretty sure it cost more than my last paycheck. The silk tickles my skin. "Oh, I'm prepared. They can be as mean and snobby and awful as they like; I won't even blink an eye, I promise."

It's supposed to be reassuring, but Sebastian's mouth flattens, and he goes back to staring out the window. His thumb taps a rapid beat against his knee.

And I don't know what comes over me—maybe I'm getting in character?—because I reach over and cover his hand with mine.

"Shitty families aren't worth stressing over. Sir," I add, remembering my place, but when I start to pull my hand back, Sebastian catches it and holds on.

"You're right." His thumb swoops over my palm, and I shiver. "But I still hate coming here."

Then why bother? I open my mouth to ask, but the car slows by the mansion entrance. Faint string music spills out of the open doors, and a big shaft of golden light spreads over the cobbles. Polite laughter trills through the air.

Staring through the car window... it's like peering into another world. Hell, another universe.

I squeeze his hand one more time then let go. "C'mon, boss. Show time."

* * *

Back in high school, I was in the theater club for a year. We put on a low-budget production of A Midsummer Night's Dream, and with the English teacher's bored tutelage, we made all the props, sewed our costumes, and learned our lines.

The show was as bad as you'd imagine, but who cares? We all had a blast, and it was better than doing whippets in the underpass with the other neighborhood kids.

I'm channeling that energy right now.

This is a role. I'm an actor in a play.

The swanky gathering out on the terrace is my stage, and this dress and these murder-heels are my costume. Sebastian Bamford is my sexy leading man, and when I laugh politely at some boring lawyer's anecdote and wind my arm through Sebastian's, I'm following the stage directions. That's all.

Bamfords bristle all around me, exchanging hard looks. They're not the whole party, but they're still everywhere. Hovering and tutting and pursing their lips.

They do not like me. Not one bit. I'm touching the crook of Sebastian's elbow, but from their horror, you'd think I just licked the side of his neck.

Oh, they greeted me in the foyer politely enough, sweeping us inside and ordering the driver to see to our bags. Sebastian's mother took the lead, flanked on either side by two aunts.

"Felicity," she said, clasping my hand between her own. Her touch was cold, and her smile didn't reach her eyes.

"Mrs Bamford." I turned my wrist, hiding the edges of my Rusty tattoo. "I'm so pleased to meet you."

"Hm," she said. "Yes, indeed."

So... yeah. That was that.

She's watching us now, staring from the next cluster of guests over. Every time I move or speak or freaking *breathe*, her shiny auburn head goes all still.

I tug on Sebastian's arm, and he leans down, tilting his head so I can murmur in his ear. A little thrill dances through me at the intimacy of that gesture, and I could get used to this role, that's for sure.

"Your mom is intense." Can she lip read? I glance over from the corner of my eye and find her staring, her grip white-knuckled on her champagne glass. "Is she going to smother me to death with a pillow while I sleep?"

"No." My boss's reply is hushed, but my racing pulse settles at the low timbre of his voice. He's always so soothing—even when work is crazy back at the office, and everyone's freaking out about deadlines, Sebastian is the calm in the storm. Best boss ever. "She'd get her staff to do that. Obviously."

Ha. "Remind me to lock my door tonight."

There's a long pause. A mix of polite chatter and classical music swells to fill the gap, and Sebastian's suit rustles as he shifts.

"*Our* door," he says at last, sounding pained. "Forgive me, I should have—but I'll sleep on the floor, Felicity. Or I could ask the staff to prepare another guest suite. Honestly, my family would be relieved; they're very traditional. Shall I—"

"No!" I tug on Sebastian's sleeve as he straightens, yanking

20

him back down. There's a shocked murmur, a loud huff from nearby. The air smells like salt and roses, and I suck in a deep breath. "Don't do that. We can share. This way you can protect me from pillow-wielding assassins, you know?"

And I'm chattering like an idiot, gripping my boss's arm like a lifeline, but inside I'm going: Aaaaaaah!

We're sharing a room this weekend? There'll only be one bed, right?

Screw sleeping on the floor. If this is my only chance, I want to feel this man's weight on the mattress next to my body, and to hear his soft, sleeping breaths up close. Want to see him all rumpled and peaceful.

Want to commit every tiny detail to memory, so I can play it over and over in my brain for the rest of my life. I'm not gonna sleep a wink tonight.

Don't care. Worth it.

Four years, okay? Four years, I've loved this man. Four years of wanting him close.

"You're sure?" Sebastian mutters. I squeeze his sleeve, scooching nearer until I'm pressed up against his side. *Stage directions. Stage directions.*

"Extra sure. I'm a method actor, sir."

He coughs out a laugh, and when he signals a nearby server for a flute of champagne—I lunge for one too. Liquid courage is exactly what I need.

The stars pulse overhead, and the well-dressed crowd mingle and laugh. I tip back my glass until tart, fizzy champagne floods my tongue, but the truth is…

I'm already giddy.

* * *

"So." It's past midnight, on the third floor of the mansion. We're in the east wing, because this place is so huge it probably has multiple zip codes. My boss stands with his back to the guest suite door, hands shoved in his pants pockets. "How would you like to handle this, Felicity?"

He looks tired. There are shadows under his eyes, and his shoulders are slumped. I don't blame him—spending time with the Bamfords should be counted in dog years. The soiree tonight only technically lasted a few hours, but it felt like a week.

But me? I'm not tired. Not at all.

The second we stepped into this room together, every nerve ending in my body zinged to life. And that rush of adrenaline had nothing to do with the swanky king sized bed or the balcony with french doors, or even the claw foot tub I can see through the doorway to the en suite.

Honestly, I'd be more comfortable on my saggy couch at home with the girls and Rusty. But being alone with my boss?

That *always* gets my heart pumping.

And maybe it's tragic to carry around this crush for years with zero encouragement; maybe I should get a new job and try to forget this man. But for this weekend at least, I'm living the dream.

Play-acting as Sebastian Bamford's girlfriend? This is my Disneyland.

Especially when he pulls his glasses off like that, rubbing his eyes with a sigh. He crosses to the bed and places them on a nightstand, like it's the most natural thing in the world; like we're an old couple with sides of the bed. It's so domestic that my heart clenches.

But then he glances around at the floor. Frowns at the plush rug, like he's trying to judge its softness.

"Don't." I grip the handle of my bag, standing on the other side of the mattress. "Just… don't, okay? Sleep in the bed."

With me.

Sebastian's mouth twists. He looks younger without the glasses; more vulnerable, even with those broad shoulders and the late night stubble shading his jaw. Hell, he's a decade older than me, and right now I want to ruffle his hair. "Is that a good idea?"

Um, it's a genius idea. The best damn idea I've ever had.

"If you sleep down there, the pillow assassins could just step right over you."

"True." His eyes crinkle as he smiles, and now that we're alone, it's the most relaxed he's looked all day. "But what if I hog the covers?"

"You can owe me an extra hour of overtime," I say. And it's meant to be a joke, meant to set him at ease, but just like that, the tension is back in his shoulders.

My boss sighs, rolling his neck, and grabs his own bag before heading for the bathroom. "That works," he says without turning his head. "Good thinking."

The door snicks shut behind him, and I bite my lip so hard it hurts.

Why did I say that? Why remind him that we're boss and assistant, nothing more?

This weekend is all I'll ever get with this man. No more self sabotage: I need to make it count.

Sebastian

Somehow, I hadn't anticipated this awkward dance: taking turns in the bathroom, negotiating sides of the bed, climbing under the covers together in tense silence. The mattress dips as I settle as far from Felicity as I can get without toppling onto the floor. I flick my lamp off and stare at the ceiling.

Her pajamas have yellow pinstripes. And such tiny shorts.

"Night, boss." Her lamp clicks off too. Felicity rustles and sighs and plumps up her pillow, and meanwhile, I stare blindly into the darkness.

It's worse with the lights off. Suddenly I hear every soft breath, every rustle of bed sheets. Her berry scent fills my lungs, unmistakable in its sweetness, and all my senses are heightened. I'm rigid with tension at the very edge of the bed.

My fists clench at my sides.

"What a day," Felicity says, like we're making conversation in the back of the car.

I grunt.

She sighs and wriggles to get comfortable.

A clock ticks somewhere in the guest suite, the pitch black darkness slowly turning to shades of gray as my eyes adjust. The drapes are shut, but moonlight filters through the sheer fabric. I've counted eighty four breaths when Felicity hums and leans over the side of the bed, rummaging in her bag.

I turn my head and watch.

In all the four years I've known her, Felicity has never become predictable. It's one of her many excellent features. Sometimes I like to play a game with myself, guessing her next move, and I'm hardly ever right.

So, what's she rummaging for? Here are my guesses: her phone. A bottle of water. An entire ham sandwich. A framed picture of her cat to place at her bedside.

My assistant settles back in the bed, and a glowing rectangle lights up. An e-reader.

Okay, then what's she reading? I need to know.

It's not like I'm going to sleep anytime soon, not with her body heat and her silky hair splayed over the pillow and the tension knotting my muscles.

This is fine. Just natural curiosity. Right?

Felicity's lying on her side, facing away from me. Her shoulder and cheek are lit up by the screen, and the sheet clings to her waist, then rises with her hip. I roll over slowly, sliding closer in a way that I hope to god is not creepy. At least she can hear me coming.

Felicity breathes steadily, tapping on the screen to turn the page. I move as close to her as I dare, propping my head on my fist, and squint over her shoulder.

Words swim into focus. I frown, temples throbbing from the strain of reading without my glasses, and it takes me a few sentences to realize what I'm reading.

I choke quietly. Pirate sex?

"This is the best part," Felicity says, tapping the screen again. "Want me to make the font bigger?"

No!

"Please," I mutter, shifting an inch closer. My head aches from squinting at the glowing screen, but I keep going. Don't even blink. "What *is* this?"

"It's called Walking His Plank."

Of course it is. Does Felicity always read this stuff? Or is this an elaborate prank to punish me for reading over her shoulder? If so, I deserve it.

Either way, I should *not* read this with my assistant. I should not lie mere inches from her body, her warmth spreading over my front, and scowl over her shoulder, one hand fisted in the sheets. I should not swallow hard as the captain lashes his captive to the mast, tying her hands behind her back, the flecks of sea spray turning her white nightgown see-through.

Is that what Felicity likes? A man who takes control? Who... bosses her around?

"Bet there are no books like this in the fancy Bamford library," she says.

I cough out a laugh. "Probably not."

"Though maybe if there were, your mom would be less uptight."

Ugh. "Felicity." I frown at the delicate shell of her ear. "That is my *mother*. Change of topic, please."

"Okay." Wait, why am I spurring this conversation on? Why am I still lying so close, my pulse thudding beneath my jaw? When Felicity turns her head slightly, her hair shifts and tickles my arm. Her eyes find mine, shining with the light of the e-reader, and I can't move. Can't breathe. Can't do anything. "Why do you keep coming here, boss? You hate it every single time."

That's true. I do.

But this is my family. And families are… complicated. Maybe the Bamford world is messed up and kind of awful, but it's the world I grew up in, the only world I've ever really known.

It's familiar. Predictable. There's comfort in that, and besides, the Bamfords are big on family loyalty. It was drilled into us as children.

"You started your own company," Felicity points out, rolling onto her back. Suddenly I'm looming over her, practically pressed up against her side, and I should shift back, but I don't. "So it's not a family firm thing."

"No," I agree. "It's not."

"And I've seen your accounts. It's not like you need an inheritance or whatever."

"You're right, I don't."

The e-reader drops face down on her stomach, cutting off the light, and suddenly we're in darkness again. Pressed together, sharing warmth. I fight to draw breath.

Wrong.

Wrong.

Wrong.

I'm crossing so many lines right now, and I can't even claim it's for our ruse. There's no one here but us. So who am I kidding, exactly?

"Then why keep coming?" Felicity asks as soft fingertips brush along my arm. She wraps a hand around my wrist and holds it, gentle and anchoring. Her thumb circles my pulse point, and she must feel when it races faster. "Why fake-date someone? Why do you care what they think?"

Why indeed. I frown into the darkness, trying to focus on her questions—a difficult feat with her touch on my skin.

My concentration is always strained when Felicity is near.

"I suppose…" My voice is gravelly. The bed creaks as I shrug. "It's the habit of a lifetime."

Pathetic, really. But Felicity hums like she understands, like she *sees* me. Her thumb draws circles on my wrist, and fuck, I've never wanted someone this badly.

To kiss her.

To flatten her into the bed.

To press her thighs apart and sink into her slick heat, preferably never to return.

Peeling away from her takes every ounce of self control I have left. I retreat to my own side of the bed, the sheets cool against my fevered skin, and I am her *boss*, damn it. Not an animal.

"Night," Felicity says.

"Sleep well."

Because *one* of us ought to—and I'm wound so tight, I may never sleep again.

Fliss

❧❦❧

"There's my beautiful boy! Oh, you're such a beautiful boy!" I coo into my phone, ignoring the scandalized stares and whispers of people walking past the gazebo. They gawp at me like I'm an animal in a zoo, never mind that in my cream dress and heels, I look like all the other fancy guests.

In fairness, no one else is gushing over an ancient cat via video chat... but that's their loss. Rusty's purr rattles through my phone speakers, and his sticky eyes fill the screen.

Somewhere in the background, the girls are watching a cooking show, but every now and then Priya's fingers come into shot, petting Rusty's brown fur.

"Is he eating well?" I call, my voice echoing across the grounds. On a nearby lawn, the guests have gathered for croquet.

Yes. Croquet.

"If you count stealing the last of the kung po chicken from under our noses, then yeah," Priya says. "He's eating like a king."

29

That's my boy. I beam at the whiskery face on the screen, heart aching with how much I love him. When we say goodbye a few minutes later, I'm breathless with missing my cat.

Sunshine beams down onto the Bamford estate, and the sky above is flawless blue. Even the snobbiest guests are more relaxed than yesterday, loosening up in the warmth. Shirt sleeves are rolled, and suit jackets slung over shoulders. Birds whistle in the trees, and the roses climbing the gazebo trellis smell like heaven.

My eyes find Sebastian, zeroing in on my broad-shouldered boss. He stands a head above everyone else in the croquet crowd, chatting dutifully with his mother. His crisp white shirt glows in the bright morning light.

Even though I'm nowhere near, Mrs Bamford keeps throwing me probing looks. Her auburn hair catches the sun each time she turns her head.

Good thing I don't give a flying rat's ass what she thinks of me.

But... Sebastian cares. He bought me fancy clothes and this watch; he coached me in etiquette. All so that people will think we're really dating, and that he made a good match. That I'm the kind of woman he'd really want.

Bleurgh.

Chewing on my bottom lip, I stroll along the garden path toward the crowd. My heels scrape against the stone, and the breeze flutters my dress against my thighs. There's a distant *smack* as a mallet hits a wooden ball.

Croquet? Seriously? How are these people real? Honestly, I thought this game was made up. Thought it only existed in Alice in Wonderland, and it's better to focus on that than the pinch of hurt that has taken up constant residence in my belly for the last week.

Whenever I remember that Sebastian needed to change me to bring me here, to present me as his girlfriend, I feel... queasy.

My normal self is not that bad. Is it?

"There you are." My boss smiles when I reach him, his eyes crinkling behind his glasses. He raises an arm, and I duck into his side like it's the most natural thing in the world.

Mrs Bamford: put out.

Sebastian's side: toasty warm and muscly beneath his shirt.

Me: smug as hell.

And we're definitely selling this fake girlfriend thing. Going the extra mile. As I watch the croquet game through the gaps in the crowd, Sebastian leans down and nuzzles my temple.

"Good phone call?" he murmurs.

"Yes." His breath tickles my cheek, and I squirm. "Rusty's fine."

"I'm glad."

God. How am I ever going to give up this intimacy now that I've felt it? How can I go back to maintaining a polite distance, never touching or teasing? When Sebastian straightens up again, I sway into the space he just occupied, chasing after his touch. I'm dazed.

"So, Sebastian." Mrs Bamford's vinegary voice jolts me back to earth. She's staring at me, her lipsticked mouth arranged in a smile. "How did the two of you meet? Seeing you with a girlfriend after all these years is just wonderful."

Ha. Yeah, right.

Bet the Bamford matriarch was only too excited to choose her son's future partner. Bet the power trip made her sweat through her fancy perfume.

"We met through work," my boss says, reeling out the story

we prepared on the car drive here. We both agreed: better to keep things simple.

So far, so terrible. There was nothing simple about sharing a bed last night. Nothing.

"Work," his mother repeats, like the very thought is distasteful.

"Yep," I say, wrapping one arm tightly around Sebastian's waist. "You know how it goes. The water cooler is a very sensual place."

My boss chokes. Mrs Bamford blinks.

"And the elevator," I go on, stroking Sebastian's ribs with my thumb. "And those networking breakfasts at 8am. All super romantic. Our eyes met over the plate of stale croissants, right Sebastian?"

"Right," he grinds out, and I can't tell if he's mad at me for running wild with our story, or trying not to laugh. Either way, his arm holds me tight to his side, so tight I can feel his heartbeat. Can he feel mine?

"Oh, my." Mrs Bamford's smile would be sweeter after sucking on a lemon. "Well, as long as you're happy..."

"I am," Sebastian says. And I'm laying it on thick, I know, but I rest my cheek against his chest. The cotton of his shirt is soft, and it smells like laundry powder and the fresh morning breeze.

Imagine it: Sebastian happy with me. Proud to call me his girlfriend. The *real* me, not this polished version dressed in someone else's clothes.

As I shift my arm, the pearl-studded watch digs into my wrist. It feels heavier this morning.

Mrs Bamford tilts her head, watching me. "After lunch, we thought we'd all take a stroll around the grounds. There are some new water features, and the two of us can chat more, Felicity. Get to know one another."

"Lovely," I say through my teeth.

An afternoon stroll with this woman? In these murder-heels? I'm toast.

* * *

Limping back toward the mansion two hours later, I'm bruised inside and out. I'm no expert, but police interrogations are probably more fun than a walk with Mrs Bamford. She grilled me on my background, my education, my political views and my hobbies. My future plans and favorite books. Needless to say, she did not coo over the photo of Rusty I showed her.

"Ow. Ow. Fuckity ow." I wait until the laughter and voices of the other guests are distant, carried away by the breeze, and then I kick off my heels. Curling my toes into the springy grass, I let out a low groan.

Never. Again.

I'm a sneakers girl from now on. Or even better: crocs. Who cares if I'll look unhinged wearing them around the office? I cannot force my blistered feet into a pair of heels for another single second.

"Felicity."

Sebastian's low voice warms me from the inside out. I huff at the grass, trying to hide the blush spreading over my cheeks.

It's always like this. My boss so much as looks at me, and I melt into a steaming puddle. I snatch the heels up from the lawn and glare at the man looming beside me.

"Your mother is a deadly weapon."

His mouth quirks. "So she is. But you clearly survived."

33

"Only just," I tell him, hobbling forward. He falls into step, never mind that I'm moving at a glacial pace. Rose bushes dot the lawn, and we weave between the sweet-smelling flowers. "For a while there, I thought she might kill me and sink my body in the ornamental fish pond."

"I doubt it." Sebastian takes my shoes, then offers his arm. I cling to his elbow, grateful for the support. "That's probably bad for the koi carp."

I hear the exact moment he notices my battered feet. His breath sucks in, and his body goes all still. My boss tugs me to a halt, staring down at my blistered toes.

Silence. A bird trills in a nearby tree, hidden by the pink and white blossom.

"Sexy, right?" I joke, uncomfortable. My toes scrunch into the grass. "I'll have to beat those retired old bankers away with a croquet mallet."

Ugh. Why now? Why does my crush have to see me like this? Why couldn't Sebastian see my bare feet when I've just got a pedicure or something, and I've slathered my whole body in essential oils?

"Felicity," my boss says, and he sounds devastated. "The shoes I picked did this?"

Kinda. Sorta.

"Walking for two hours with your mom did this." In these shoes.

Sebastian drags his free hand down his face, then glares at the heels clutched in his fist. He looks ready to fling them into the stratosphere.

"They're pretty," I assure him quickly. "Well, I mean, they're not my style, but they were a good pick for this weekend—"

"No, they weren't." The heels land beneath the nearest rose

bush with two soft thuds. Hopefully some lucky gardener thinks to sell them on eBay, because they're worth a small fortune, even stained with my blood. "Come here."

The sky tilts, and my breath seizes, and then I'm in my boss's arms. Cradled against his chest like something precious, never mind that carrying your girlfriend is probably *not done* on this estate.

"They're gonna gossip about this," I warn. My arms slide around his neck, and Sebastian's so warm and sturdy. The grass blurs beneath his long strides.

"I don't care," he says.

"They already think I'm a ragamuffin."

"Fliss? I don't care."

I grin at my boss, suddenly a million times lighter. His face is close to mine, and he's holding me so steady I barely feel the motion of his steps.

The air changes. Gets cooler. Sebastian's footsteps echo across the marble foyer, and in a distant room, piano keys tinkle.

"You can't carry me to our suite in the middle of the day. They'll think you want a nooner."

"It's two thirty."

"You're missing the point."

My boss sighs, carrying me up the stairs like I'm made of feathers. He's scowling behind his glasses, and his bronze hair has been ruffled by the breeze.

I bite my lip, trying to commit every detail of this moment to memory.

His strong arms holding me up.

His warm chest, so muscly beneath his shirt.

The soap and basil scent of his neck.

"We're going to our room, and I'm going to tend your feet. This is not a discussion, Felicity."

Whelp. No arguments here.

Sebastian

Thirty minutes later, I carry my assistant back downstairs, her feet bathed and treated and wrapped up in a pair of thick's men's hiking socks I found at the bottom of my bag.

"They're clean," I promise her for the dozenth time as we descend the stairs.

Felicity grins, gently tugging the hairs at the back of my neck. "I know. I sniffed them when you weren't looking."

Ha. Well, I can hardly blame her.

And she seems… fine. Not at all traumatized by her morning walk with my mother, or by her poor, shredded feet, or by spending a night in the same bed with her boss.

The worst boss in the world, clearly. How can I ever make all this up to her?

"These fancy house parties are so intense," Felicity whispers as I carry her through the mansion corridors, trying not to rumple her cream dress. The last thing we need is the Bamfords tutting over creases in her skirt. "It's like you go non stop, and not in a fun way. When does everyone catch their breath? Get a minute to themselves?"

"Privacy is for wimps."

My assistant snorts, and her fingers are still in my hair. It takes every ounce of my willpower not to buck into her touch like a cat, purring like a madman.

Piano music drifts through the halls. I follow the sound to a reception room on the ground floor, where priceless chintzy armchairs are scattered around a grand piano and servers stand by with pots of steaming tea.

We've found the old people's room, then. No one in here is younger than eighty. They all sag in the armchairs in tailored suits and dresses, some smiling dreamily at the pianist, some napping. I scan the tufts of white hair, looking for a spare seat.

Perfect. Felicity wants a minute of peace? This is as close to a break we're going to get.

"Sebastian," my grandmother coos when I lower Felicity into the armchair beside her. "You've brought your lady friend to meet us!"

Or not.

Because as the nearest white-tufted heads swivel and my grandmother pierces us with her blue eyes, it feels more like we've wandered into the lions' den.

"Ah." Plumping the cushions, I force my brain back into gear. Fake girlfriend. Family deception. Right. "Yes, this is Felicity. Felicity, this is my grandmother, Maude."

"Nice to meet you." My assistant waves. There are a few murmurs; a harsh sigh in the corner. Someone snores at the back of the room. And after a few minutes of chatting, the heads have all turned away.

All except my grandmother.

She watches me, eyes big and round like an owl, and her hand is gnarled with arthritis where she grips her teacup. The pianist plays beautifully, but my grandmother is deaf to it.

"You met at work?"

"Yes, we did."

She hums, and sucks on her false teeth. Then: "I met your grandfather at work, you know. I was a typist in his office. Kissed the daylights out of him, right there in the staff coat room."

Felicity spares me from reacting to that, thank god. She clutches her chest and gives this big, dramatic sigh, but the strange thing is… I don't think she's faking.

"Tell me everything," Felicity says. "What was he like? Did you have a crush on him right away?"

We're hit by a cloud of lily of the valley perfume as the old lady leans closer.

"Percy was a *stallion*, dear. With terribly broad shoulders, and a very masculine, bristly mustache. When he kissed me, my legs turned to jelly."

Felicity sighs and smiles.

Hm. Should I grow a mustache?

"I've never heard that story before," I say. So many years of chatting with my grandmother, and I never knew how she met her husband. Surreal.

She wheezes a laugh. "Well, it's hardly Bamford fare, is it? No, it was quite the scandal back then. They all thought I was miles beneath him. A typist, and a girl from his office? Oh, no. Took them years to warm up to me. Poor cousin Edgar had to have his meltdown before they'd turn their focus elsewhere."

My assistant fiddles with the corner of a cushion. She's completely absorbed by this conversation, practically forgetting

I'm here.

Soft music drifts through the room. My legs ache from kneeling beside her armchair, but I don't get up. Not yet.

"But your husband didn't care?" Felicity asks. "He loved you anyway?"

My grandmother pats her hand. "He did. Maybe even a little extra. Men love a challenge, you know."

Oh?

Felicity glances at my raised eyebrow and smiles. Then pure mischief flits over her beautiful face.

She leans toward the older woman. "Sebastian would never kiss me at the office," she confides. "Sometimes all I want is for him to ravage me against the copier, but he'll never do it." Her eyes are fixed on me, sparking with challenge.

This is fake, I remind myself. She's teasing me, that's all. She's always loved to tease.

But fuck, my body heats at her words, and my hands itch to plunge into her silky hair.

"Well, that's no use," my grandmother says. "Can't you coax him out of his shell? My grandson was always rather shy, you know."

Felicity shrugs. "I've tried everything. I wear the skirts I know he likes; I rub his shoulders when he gets tense. I'm at a loss, Maude. Next thing I'll be draped over his desk, fully nude with an apple in my mouth."

Jesus Christ.

My knees crack as I lurch to my feet. "Tea," I declare, head spinning as I look for a server. "I'll get us tea."

She *does* rub my shoulders sometimes when I'm stressed. How much of this is real? I stagger toward the nearest server in a daze.

40

For god's sake. This is ridiculous.

I'm losing track of my own con.

* * *

The piano music ends after another hour or so, and the more sprightly members of the audience shuffle back out into the corridor. My grandmother winks at us before hobbling away, and I lift Felicity into my arms then leave the napping octogenarians behind.

"What's next?" my assistant murmurs, her arms wrapped around my neck. She offered to walk, said she could manage it in the hiking socks, etc, etc, but obviously I won't allow that. Our faces are close, her breath tickling my cheek, and my steps drum against the marble tiles. "A vineyard tour? Afternoon drinks on a private yacht?"

"More lawn games, I believe."

Her snort ruffles the hair by my ear. "What a rager."

She has no idea.

This has been my life. My whole childhood. And Felicity joked with my grandmother, but frankly I'm shocked that I'm not more repressed than I am.

If I was more normal, if I didn't have all this family baggage… would I have kissed her by now? Would she have let me? I'm starting to think she might.

What a bittersweet thought.

It's late afternoon, the sunshine buttery and warm. Guests drift over the rolling lawns, winding their way toward yet another polite gathering near the terrace. Strained laughter trills through the air.

The grass is soft beneath my feet. And duty has always come

easily for me, has always been automatic, but as I carry my assistant toward the gathering—my pulse spikes, and I veer left.

"Um," Felicity says, as I march toward the hedge maze. I'm moving faster now, gripping her tight against my chest. "Where are we going?" She sucks in a thrilled breath. "Are we playing hooky?"

"We are."

"In a hedge maze?" The air is cooler in here, and everything is tinged blue where the sunshine can't reach. I carry Felicity through the leafy corridors, my pulse calming.

It smells like soil and greenery, and the faint fruity scent of her shampoo. She's so warm, so soft in my arms. A bird flutters in the hedge.

My steps slow. "I panicked. We can go back if you like."

"No!" Her hold tightens on my neck. "No, I like it in here. What's in the middle? What do we get if we solve it?"

"A fountain, I think. And a few moments alone."

"Peeeerfect."

And it warms me down to my bones to hear her say that. To feel how relaxed she is in my arms. By rights, Felicity should hate me by now, but if anything she burrows closer.

The tip of her nose is cool against my throat. "Are you cold?" I rasp, hitching her higher against my chest.

"A bit." Her fingertips slide between my shirt buttons, coasting over my bare chest, and I nearly stagger into the hedge. Out of nowhere, I'm half hard. "You can warm me up at the fountain."

"Oh?"

"If you want to."

I would literally chop a limb off if it meant I could touch this

42

woman. Clearing my throat, I pick up the pace again, solving the maze by memory. It's been a few years, but the stakes have never been higher.

"You're good at this," Felicity says after several minutes.

"I'm suddenly very motivated."

Her soft laughter trails us through the foliage.

Fliss

❧

This maze feels like something out of a myth. You know: towering green hedges, roots twining through the packed dirt, birds rustling and a distant blue sky overhead. Though we're not super far from the lawn games, we can't hear a peep from the other guests.

It's just me, my boss, and our rasping breaths.

He solves the maze almost on the first try. With the couple of wrong turns he takes, he curses like a sailor under his breath then backtracks, jaw clenched. It's so unlike him—so uncontrolled.

Sebastian's muscles are tense. His heartbeat slams against my side.

Using my fingertip, I nudge his glasses up the bridge of his nose.

"Thank you," he mutters.

When we spill into the center of the maze, I suck in a wobbly breath. It's even more otherworldly in here, with a fountain spraying crystal-clear water and stone tiles forming a mini

44

terrace in the shaft of sunlight. Two statues frolic in the water, frozen in their poses: a satyr and a nymph. They are wearing the tiniest scraps of carved cloth.

"You know, that satyr's pretty ripped," I say.

"Don't make me jealous of a statue, Felicity. Have mercy."

There are two wrought iron benches, but Sebastian carries me right to the fountain. He sits me down on the stone wall, then kneels at my feet.

"Your blisters?" A strong hand wraps around my ankle, and lifts my foot like I'm delicate. My boss rubs the arch of my foot, and I choke back a groan. That should *not* feel so good.

"They're fine," I grit out. "I haven't walked a single step since you checked them before. You can't carry me for this whole weekend, you know."

"Of course I can." Sebastian lifts a shoulder. His white shirt strains against his muscles. "You're my girlfriend, remember?"

...Right.

This is make-believe. A weekend of weaving our own private myth.

But even though we're alone here, with no one else to impress or convince, my boss doesn't move away. And maybe he's a method actor too—maybe he wants to stay in our roles.

Fine by me. Disneyland, baby.

Sebastian swaps to my other foot, rubbing his thumb over my sore arch. Shuddering out a sigh, I tip my head back and let my eyes flutter closed.

"Felicity."

"It's Fliss," I tell him for the millionth time.

A long pause.

"Fliss, then." Clever fingers smooth over my foot, my ankle, my bare calf. They trail all the way up to my knee, whisper-light, and I'm so freaking glad I shaved my legs this morning.

My thighs part an inch. My teeth dig into my bottom lip.

Nerves squirm in my belly, and our stolen sunshine licks over my skin. It's shockingly nice after the cool, dark maze.

Sebastian places a steady palm on my leg. "Would you still like me to warm you up?"

I nod so fast my teeth clack together. And my eyes are still closed, but I hear his smoky laugh; I sense him shift closer, tiny stones crunching under his knees.

His hand slides an inch higher. The thumb strokes inward, tickling my inner thigh, and I can't breathe. Can't breathe.

Squeezing the stone lip of the fountain, I wait, silently begging for more. He won't stop now, will he? That would be so cruel.

Silence. Stillness.

I blink my eyes open and find Sebastian watching me.

His mouth curves up. "There you are," he says. And the way his eyes glitter... the hungry look on his face...

It's nothing like my stern boss from real life. That man barely looked at me twice in four years; he'd never have broken the strict rules and regulations of the office and beyond.

But *this* man looks ready to devour me whole. His chest heaves beneath his white shirt, and his pulse thuds visibly beneath his jaw. The hand on my leg sears my skin.

This is still fake, right? Still a game. It has to be. Because if I get my hopes up, then it all goes back to normal...

Well, I'll shrivel into a dried husk. A dehydrated lump of Fliss, so crispy and small that Rusty can bat me around the kitchen floor. Simple as that.

"So," Sebastian says. "You want me to ravage you against the copier."

My throat is tight, but when I speak, it sounds almost normal. Only a tiny bit strangled. "Here works too."

My boss laughs, and I still don't recognize him like this. So carefree. As he leans forward, I meet him partway, and...

...Bliss.

That's how it feels when our lips brush. Like the warm, bright sunshine has sunk through my skin and is inside me now too, spreading like liquid gold through my veins. I'm glowing. Gasping.

Sebastian makes a low noise, and our mouths slant together harder. My nose squishes against his cheek. His teeth tug my lip.

Holy shit.

This is what heaven feels like. This is what you get if you're good your whole life and you never step too far wrong: Sebastian Bamford cupping your neck with one hand and squeezing your thigh with the other, kissing you like a starving man.

Or maybe that's just me. Other people can have different fantasies, I guess.

But they're all wrong.

"Wait," my boss mutters, pulling away, and my belly drops. He regrets it already, doesn't he? God, that was too short. Too tantalizing. But no: Sebastian plucks his glasses off and places them nearby on the wall, then crowds closer again. His hand slips higher, nudging under my dress.

"You," he tells me between kisses, "taste so—fucking sweet. I knew you would."

Well, I knew he'd be all bossy and delicious. Guess we've both won the jackpot today.

It takes a second to unclench my fingers from the stone wall, my brain all muddled by his kiss, but then I take his wrist. Tug his hand closer to the juncture of my thighs, rucking up my skirt as we go.

"If you want." I kiss him hard, head spinning. "You can touch me here if you want."

Sebastian curses and crowds even closer, wedging my thighs on either side of his hips. "Of course I fucking want to. Are you kidding, Fliss? I've wanted to touch you since the first day we met."

He has?

That… doesn't sound fake. It doesn't match our cover story. And if we're breaking our roles, then I have a few confessions too.

The fountain burbles behind me, and I reach for his belt. Yank it open, leather creaking as he pushes my dress up around my hips. My heart's beating so fast right now.

"I've thought about a few things too, Mr B. Like riding you in your office chair, creasing up your fancy clothes. Or sucking you off beneath the desk while you're on the phone to your rich guy contacts. Or pulling the emergency brake in the elevator and bending over in front of the mirror for you."

Sebastian snarls, wrenching my underwear down my thighs. He gets my panties as far as my parted legs will allow, then leans forward and sucks a harsh kiss on my neck.

Yeah, I'm very imaginative for a virgin. Or maybe it's *because* I've never hooked up that I have so many lurid daydreams. All that pent up longing's gotta go somewhere, you know? And up until now, it's fueled the porn reel of Sebastian and I—the one playing in a constant loop in my brain.

"You're going to give me a heart attack," my boss says against my heated skin. His fingertips delve between my thighs, coasting along my slit, and he groans when he finds me soaked. "*Fliss*. Ah, god. Fuck."

"It's for you," I babble, and it's probably a lame thing to say, but it's true. "It's all for you." His thumb finds my clit and I arch back with a cry, and I'm spinning out of control—spinning right out of my body.

Only one thing anchors me. His rough voice; his stern touch. *Sebastian*. Is this really happening?

"That's right." Those gray eyes are extra stormy. This man is so big, so strong, surrounding me, *owning* me. His bronze hair is ruffled, and a flush has spread over his cheekbones. "You're mine, Felicity. Mine."

Gah. I wish!

When he presses one finger inside me, I grit my teeth against a moan. Sebastian rubs circles over my clit, and I bite down on his shoulder. And it's uncouth of me—the Bamfords would tut themselves into early graves if they knew—but then, they'd hate everything about this, wouldn't they? Especially the wild glint in my boss's eye.

Liquid heat pools low in my belly, and sensations prickle over my skin. Every touch from him, every kiss and grunt and curse, makes me shiver.

Somehow, I remember how to move my hands. With my forehead pressed against my boss's throat, with one of his hands between my legs and the other sliding into my dress to cup my breast, I reach down between us and work his pants open.

"You don't have to." His low voice is rough. Strained. It sounds so loud compared to the hush of the fountain and the twittering birds.

"I want to." He presses a second finger inside me, and I nip his throat in reply.

So full. So good.

So perfect.

I'm stretched tight, but it's not enough. One day soon, I want *all* of him. Would he ever allow that? From the things he's been saying… maybe he would.

If I could even take him.

"Damn, sir." I whistle as I draw his cock out, weighing the heavy shaft in my palm. It's either joke or run away babbling at this point, because he's thick and long and veined and *god*.

I'm so ill-equipped for this moment. And this is my *boss*.

Don't care. I'm forging ahead anyway.

"Yes." Sebastian hisses through his teeth as I stroke him. "Harder, Fliss. Yes, that's right."

His fingers slide along my slit, teasing and torturing. They pump inside me, crooking against my inner walls.

And we're both breathing in short gasps. Both burning up together, so hot under our clothes that we're creating our own micro climate in the center of this maze. It's extra humid, extra warm, the air so close.

The fountain mists the backs of my shoulders. When I reach down to fondle his balls, Sebastian kisses me so hard that spots of light float behind my eyes.

And this is…

An explosion. Four years' worth of pent up tension and desire, finally releasing all in one go. Our hands move faster, become clumsy, and as we both lock up and shudder, muscles twitching…

It's a brave new world. Heat roars through my body, my heart shuddering, and I swear for a split second, I see sounds.

Meanwhile, my boss comes on my thigh with a tortured

groan, lashing my bare skin. It's warm and sticky and pearly white. Definitely gonna tease him for that later, even if it's so hot I can't stand it.

Next time I want him to paint my bare stomach. Or my boobs. Or my pussy. Or, no, screw it, my *insides*—

Because I'm his, and this man owns me. Always has.

But sometimes being head-over-heels for someone isn't enough, and Sebastian's glasses scrape against the fountain wall as he picks them up. Once they're safely back on his nose, he frowns at my rumpled hair, my creased dress, the spend on my thigh. His jaw ticks, and it's like he's seeing clearly again, his mood souring.

My heart sinks. The fountain mist is suddenly freezing.

Didn't he like it? Those were the best minutes of my life.

"We'll need to clean up before dinner," my boss mutters, pushing to his feet. "Get you Bamford-ready again."

Uh-huh. The punch of hurt makes it hard to breathe, because outside this maze, he wants the fake Fliss. Not *me*. How did I forget that?

As he scoops me into his arms, I'm stiff and cold. A sad little corpse in a stained fancy dress.

How did I fool myself so badly? I'm such an idiot.

Sebastian

My assistant is rigid, her expression strained. Each second of her clear misery pushes me lower. What the hell have I done? What was I thinking, touching her like that?

Kissing her and putting my hands on her body? Showing her my goddamn cock? I'm her *boss*.

And an animal.

A complete disgrace.

Those were the best minutes of my life, but that's no excuse. The price of being in charge is putting everyone else first, and Fliss, above all others, is my top priority.

Her comfort and safety. Her happiness.

She stares at my shoulder, chin wobbling, and fuck. I want to die.

"Forgive me," I say as I carry her back through the maze. It's like holding a stack of firewood, she's so stiff and unyielding. "I shouldn't have done that, Felicity."

Her laugh is pained. "No, I guess you shouldn't, sir."

But I'm weak. I let my instincts get the better of me. I've wanted this woman for so long, and she seemed to want me too, and I…

I bought into our ruse. Forgot we were playing roles.

It's darker between the hedges now—the evening sky is bruised overhead, and the light's draining fast. I squint at the shadowed dirt, stepping over half-buried roots. A bird rustles between the leaves as we pass, and it smells like damp soil and old stone.

How do I fix this? How do I make her smile again?

"I think I'll walk from here."

"But your feet—"

"It's fine." Fliss pokes my shoulder like she's jabbing the button to get off the city bus. "Down, please."

Ugh. Damn it.

The instant those hiking socks hit the ground, she scuttles away and puts space between us. We walk through the rest of the maze so far apart, her shoulder drags along the hedge. Birds chatter furiously as she ruffles up their leaves.

I'm such a jackass. Can't believe I did this.

And I'm *definitely* sleeping on the floor tonight.

* * *

Here's an understatement: the last thing I want to do right now is have a stuffy Bamford dinner. I'd rather be at home in my apartment, slamming my forehead against the granite counter tops. Or better yet, pulling one of those rare late nights at the office with Fliss, when she orders us both take-out from her favorite weird restaurants and tells me stories about her cat.

She's been the light of my life for so long. And now she's

dimmed, and it's my fault.

"Felicity," my mother says from two seats down, leaning around a guest to stare at my fake girlfriend. "Is there a problem with the food? Would you like something different?"

My assistant forces a polite smile. She's been chasing a cube of feta around her plate with a fork. "Not at all, Mrs Bamford. Everything is delicious."

Delicious and boring. If our stuffy old chef ever met a spice, he'd die of fright.

I chew slowly, watching Fliss across the table. She's in a green cocktail dress, her feet in Greek sandals beneath the table, and she's fixed her hair again. It's pinned up in a staid bun, all the pink streaks hidden.

My chest throbs.

She looks so tired. Exhausted by what I've put her through. Her hazel eyes are shadowed, and her shoulders curve forward.

My mother is not helping matters. "Goodness," she says, craning her perfumed neck for a better look. "Is that a tattoo on your wrist?"

Fliss blinks down at the tips of Rusty's ears where they poke out beneath her watch. Her eyebrows pinch together, like she forgot the tattoo was even there. The fork droops in her hand.

"It hardly matters," I say as Fliss places her fork on the table. Then, directly to my assistant: "You don't need to show them."

Screw it. She doesn't owe these people anything.

My mother huffs. Dozens of eyes stare as Fliss undoes the watch clasp.

It lands heavily on the table cloth. Fliss holds up her wrist, tilting it left and right to show the whole table.

"This is my cat, Rusty. He drools when he purrs."

All along the table, hands flutter over chests, and scandalized whispers break out. For god's sake. It's just a tiny tattoo.

And how have these people been so sheltered their whole lives? How are they so easily perturbed? It's pathetic, frankly, and I'm abruptly so annoyed that I pandered to them at all. That I made Fliss cover her tattoo over in the first place.

I don't deserve this woman.

My fingers clench around my fork. My throat is so tight.

"I like it," I say loudly, and three seats away, an aunt gasps like I just declared a whipped cream fetish.

My mother scoffs. "Well, no Bamford will ever have such a thing."

"If I marry Felicity, a Bamford clearly will."

If she took my name, anyway. Whatever, it's hypothetical, and now my cheeks are hot. I squeeze my knife and fork tighter to keep from tugging at my collar, and ignore my startled mother.

Fliss blinks at me across the fancy dinner settings. She looks baffled, but…

Lighter, maybe. Hopeful.

I suck in my first deep breath since the maze.

"I have one too, actually," my grandmother quavers down the table. She's hunched over her soup bowl, her puffy white hair like a tiny cloud. I swear, when she meets my eye, she winks at me. "But I couldn't show it here. It's not suitable for the dinner table. My Percy loved it."

Louder murmurs this time. Wine glasses are snatched up and raised to trembling lips.

Fliss beams at my grandmother down the table. "I bet he did, Maude." I've known that woman all my life, but somehow these two have built a closer bond in a single afternoon. Bizarre.

Something brushes against my ankle under the table. Felicity's foot.

I swallow hard, staring so hard at my assistant that my eyes go dry. Don't want to blink. Don't want her to move her foot away.

Don't want to fuck this up again. I'll die if I do.

* * *

My grandmother corners me on the terrace after dinner. The doors to the dining room have been thrown wide, and a violinist plays inside, the music floating out into the starry night. My mother's guests mill around, laughing politely, chatting about golf and politics and—let's face it—Felicity. They can't decide whether they're thrilled or offended by her free spirit, but give them time. No one can resist Fliss for long.

Now, where has my assistant gone?

"There you are."

My grandmother moves so slowly, I drain the last of my scotch and signal for two waters before she arrives. I swear, she gets smaller and more hunched over each time I see her.

I should visit more often. Visit *her*, anyway. The rest of the Bamfords…

Well, maybe I don't care what they think after all. Anyone who dislikes Fliss clearly has awful taste, and their opinion is worthless to me.

"You've found a lovely girl," my grandmother says when she finally reaches me. The top of her head is just above my elbow. I hand her a glass of water, and it clinks against her wedding ring. "So much nicer than the one your mother picked out."

She actually picked someone out? Her schemes went that far? No wonder she's been prickly about Fliss from the moment we

56

arrived. I've thrown an assistant-sized spanner in her works.

"I don't need a matchmaker."

"Quite," my grandmother agrees.

"It's so controlling."

"Well, the Bamfords do love to keep us in line." It takes one hundred years for her to sip her drink. Her wrinkly throat moves as she swallows. "It's no way to live, though. When they told my Percy to marry someone else, he told them all to go to hell. We eloped to Italy. It was terribly romantic, and you couldn't just hop on a plane in those days, Sebastian—we crossed an ocean to be together. And to escape the Bamfords for a while," she adds with a twinkle. "I'm sure you understand."

I certainly do. In fact: "Why come back at all?" If I coaxed Fliss to the Mediterranean, I'm not sure I'd ever return. It'd be sun, sea and pasta into eternity.

My grandmother wheezes a laugh. "I could ask you the same question, my boy. Well, I suppose because they're not so bad once they've given up hope of controlling you. Your mother can be rather fun when she lets herself relax—and I like the gardens, of course. Did you and Felicity enjoy the hedge maze together?"

She saw us go in there? Did anyone else?

Ugh. Who cares?

"Maybe too much," I admit.

"Or not enough." A bony elbow digs into my side. "Loosen up, Sebastian. You've got your whole life to stomp around and scowl."

Isn't that the awful truth? "They'll bug you about that tattoo, you know." Sure, I'm grateful for her distraction, but my grandmother will pay dearly for it.

"Sweetheart?" She pats my arm. "I'm eighty seven. I don't

give a shit."

Fliss

❦

This has been a *day*. A long, tense, confusing day on this fancy estate where I don't belong and I'm not welcome. My emotions have been buffeted around by gale force winds; I've reached the highest highs then plummeted to the lowest lows.

There's only one thing for it: a video call with Priya and Rusty.

I sneak back to our suite after dinner, tiptoeing through the corridors in my sandals. Heavy gilt frames line the mansion walls, filled with burnished mirrors and oil paintings of landscapes. Everything on this estate is priceless.

What was it like for Sebastian, growing up here? Bet he couldn't play or run or whoop. Bet he couldn't invite friends over—unless they were pre-approved. No wonder he's so buttoned down.

Although...

He seemed looser at dinner. Rougher around the edges, jumping to my defense—and his mom even cornered me on the terrace after dessert and *apologized*. Forced the words out between her teeth, but still. I swallow hard, and my tongue is thick in my mouth.

None of it means anything. I can't get my hopes up.

The suite is hushed when I slip inside. I close the door, kick off my sandals, and pad over to the bed—and last night already feels like a million years ago. I pause, heart hammering, and rest my fingertips on the bed covers as I call up the memory: Sebastian's heat behind me, the mattress dipping with his weight. His low voice in my ear. The warm, gooey feeling in my belly as we read Walking His Plank.

Oof.

With a little shake, I snatch up my phone from the nightstand. Two seconds later, I'm propped against the headboard as it rings.

"Fliss?"

Priya sounds harried, her phone pointed at our kitchen ceiling, probably left on the counter. Clattering noises say she's cooking dinner.

"Hey. Just calling to check in." And to see my fluffy baby if he's around. Priya grunts, and my roomie knows me so well, because she comes into frame then lowers the phone to the floor.

"There ya go."

A whiskery face comes into view, snuffling at Priya's camera. Rusty's purr thrums through the phone speakers.

"There's my handsome prince!"

I know I sound insane. But I don't care, because Rusty has *never* messed with my emotions or made me feel all fluttery and unhinged. He's a very straightforward cat.

I feed him; he loves me. The rules of our relationship are

clear.

"How are the Boring Bamfords?" Priya's voice is distant, echoing across the kitchen. I shrug, though she can't see me.

"Stuffy as hell."

"Gross," she says. "Hope that boss of yours pays you extra overtime."

I cringe, tapping the phone screen with a fingernail. Does an orgasm in a hedge maze count? I forgot I was being paid for this weekend. Rusty bucks his head against the phone, like I'm really petting him—and he blocks out Priya's words, but when she filters back in, my stomach churns.

"...can't believe you've loved this guy for years."

"Hey, you think *your* boss is hot."

"I said he's handsome," she corrects, knocking a spoon against a pan. Rusty purrs and drools on the camera, smudging the image. "You know, objectively speaking. But I'm not attracted to him at all. Although—"

She cuts off, slamming a drawer shut.

Uh-huh.

"You're telling me everything when I get home."

"Likewise." The suite door opens and Sebastian slips inside, and I don't have time to warn Priya before she says, "Now go screw your grumpy boss so you have some good stories."

I splutter, cheeks flushing.

Rusty meows.

Sebastian raises an eyebrow.

"Gotta go," I rush out, hanging up, but the damage is done. He's standing there, all tall and broody and knowing. His bronze hair is pushed back from his forehead, and with his muscles and that jawline, he could be one of the statues on a plinth in the gardens.

Sebastian slides his hands into his pockets, then strolls forward to the edge of the bed.

"That was Rusty," I say.

My boss hums. "Your cat is salacious."

"And my roommate Priya."

The faintest smile. "I see."

He's not mad? My phone thunks against the nightstand, and I draw my knees up, twiddling my thumbs next to my chest. This bed is so huge that I'm lost in an ocean of high thread count sheets.

What is he thinking? Is he obsessing over what happened in the maze too? Has he moved on already? What happened back there at dinner?

Aaah!

"I don't want overtime," I blurt. Sebastian tilts his head, waiting for me to go on, and those gray eyes are like the winter ocean. "I don't want you to pay me for this. It's—it's weird."

"Alright," he agrees slowly. "Then I don't want it to be fake."

I turn to stone, going rigid against the headboard. "You...you don't?"

"No," he says. "I don't."

Hands still in his pockets, my boss comes around the bed to my side. My ears are ringing. My face is numb. He wants this to be real? I want that so badly, my insides are all churned up like the soil in the flower beds outside.

"For this weekend?" Maybe it's still a method actor thing.

"For the rest of our lives. You know," Sebastian adds with a crooked smile, sinking down to sit by my leg, "if you can tolerate me for that long."

The bed creaks under his weight, and this makes no sense. This isn't how things go between us!

He's the icy, distant, unreachable boss, and I'm the lovesick assistant who pines for him every night in her pajamas. Those are our real roles, and I'm used to them. They're comfortable. Familiar.

Safe.

This isn't safe. This is standing in one of those plane doorways, thousands of feet above the ground, hoping against hope that my parachute works. Oh, and the plane is on fire.

"Fliss," Sebastian says gently. His gray eyes are so kind. "You don't have to agree. I'm not ordering you as your boss, I'm... entreating you. As a man."

My heart thumps against my ribs. "Entreating?"

His nose wrinkles. "I couldn't think of the right word."

"You sound like Mr Darcy."

"And you don't like that?"

"No, I do."

It takes every ounce of my courage—which is ridiculous, when you consider our antics in the maze—but I raise both hands and force my fingers to uncurl. His glasses slide easily off his nose, and I place them on my nightstand right next to my e-reader.

My breath empties out at the sight of our possessions side by side. "I've always wanted to do that."

And he leans forward, already reaching for me—already *kissing* me, hands gently cupping my neck. The guest suite blurs around us, and he's so warm and sturdy. His mouth is demanding, moving firmly over mine.

"*Mmph.*" I kiss him back, though I'm completely addled. Don't know which way is up, and his shirt strains in my grip.

This is perfect. It's everything I've wanted for so long. His soap and basil scent wraps around me, and I'm falling, falling,

falling.

Then reality kicks back in, and I tear my mouth away. I'm out of the plane now, plummeting toward the earth, and the little buildings and trees down there are getting bigger. This is gonna hurt. "Wait, what about work? And your family? What about—"

Sebastian pushes me down to the bed with a snarl. "Whatever you want," he grinds out, rubbing his flushed cheek against mine. His toned body is heavy, but I don't mind. Want him to squish me into blissful oblivion. "Whatever makes you happy and comfortable, Fliss. I'll do anything, alright? The rest is details. I'm yours."

Parachute: open.

The view up here: freaking beautiful.

"Okay," I wobble out, hooking my legs around his hips. My head's jammed at a weird angle from the headboard, but I sincerely do not care. "Okay then. Let's do this thing."

"Yeah?" He looks so hopeful. So *vulnerable*. My heart cracks open, and I loop my arms around his neck.

"Yeah."

Sebastian rears back. He grabs my ankles and yanks me to the center of the bed. My boss grips both sides of my neckline in his fists, then tears the cocktail dress clean down the middle and wrenches the scraps from under me.

Um.

What?!

I blink up at him, stunned and so turned on. Cool air washes over my bare skin, goosebumps ripple down my arms and stomach, and I can't stop shifting my hips. I'm needy suddenly, all hot and squirmy and so desperate for his touch.

His manly, dress-destroying touch. Yowza.

"Dude, you bought that dress. You know how expensive it was."

Sebastian tosses the green scraps of fabric to the rug. They flutter out of sight. "Money well spent."

I grab his hands and put them on my hips. "You're insane."

And nuts he may be, but Sebastian Bamford strips us both in record time, flinging clothes around the suite; he shoves my legs apart and buries his face between my thighs like there's a dessert buffet down there.

"Holy—!" My back bows; I clench the covers so hard my fingers ache. He licks me, sucks me, *devours* me, his evening stubble scraping against my inner thighs, and I can't do anything except buck and howl.

We're going to bring down this fancy mansion. We're going to drown out the stuffy string music. We're going to—

"Stop it," Sebastian growls, his words vibrating against my clit. "Stop overthinking, Fliss."

Can't help it. Now I *really* don't want the people here to hate me. "Am I being too loud?"

He squeezes my hips so hard I whimper. "Not loud enough. Come here," he says, and slings my thigh over his shoulder, then plunges his tongue inside me, and it's hot and slick and so intimate I can't breathe.

He's *good* at this.

Who knew I wanted him to be stern with my pussy? Well. He did, I guess.

"Enough," I say, once I can work my mouth again. Tugging on fistfuls of bronze hair, I drag my boss up my body. He comes reluctantly, his lips and chin slick, hands sinking into the mattress either side of my head. "Enough. I'm going to come if you keep doing that—"

A pointed look. "That is very much the goal."

"—And I want you inside me the first time. I want you to feel it too."

Sebastian pauses. Stares down at me like he wants to absorb this moment, to commit every detail to memory. He strokes my hair, gone all sweet again, and his gray eyes rove over my features.

"It might hurt the first time. *Your* first time."

He picked up on that, huh? I shrug, bed covers rustling. "Don't care. I want you."

Sebastian's forehead drops down, and his exhale is shaky. "Ah, Fliss. I'll never deserve you."

Then he shifts to line our hips up; he reaches between us, jaw clenched.

I pepper soft kisses along his cheekbone.

Sebastian

It's really hard to concentrate when she does that. And really hard to be a gentleman in this moment when all my instincts are screaming for me to thrust inside my beautiful assistant and *rut*.

But Fliss has always had this effect on me. She pushes the primal buttons in my brain. Something about her mischievous smile and hazel eyes makes me want to sling her over my shoulder, carry her home to my cave, then fuck her and love her and bring her woolly mammoth for breakfast every day.

Still, I never thought we'd be *here*. Both nude—heated, bare skin against skin—with her hair spread in a tangle over the bed sheets and her lips trailing across my cheek.

I sift through her hair until I find a raspberry streak. Spread it out on the covers and make sure I can see it.

That's better. It's been awful, seeing Fliss all buttoned-up and toned down for my family. What was I thinking?

"You're sure?" I settle in the cradle of her thighs, the head of my cock probing her entrance. I'm so hard my gut aches.

Want her. Need her.

"Fliss?"

She stops kissing my cheek and flops back. Her eyes are glassy. "Of course I'm sure, dumbass. I've loved you for four years."

She has?

My chest burns. I'm not worthy, but then no man ever could be, so… guess I'll take my lottery win and run with it.

"I've loved you every day too." The words scrape out of my throat, and I thrust into the first inch of her channel. She hisses, thighs hitching around my waist. "We're idiots, Fliss."

"Tell me about it."

She's tensed up, braced for pain. And that's no good, so I snake a hand between us and tease her clit, rubbing in steady circles until she finally melts against the mattress again, her cheeks bright pink.

"Oh, god." She rocks up into my touch, nudging me deeper. She's slicker already, her body softening, and I lick her throat. She's salty. "Oh, *god*."

"That's it," I murmur, muscles vibrating with restraint. "Let me in, sweetheart. Show me you're mine."

Fliss whimpers.

My heart raps out a triumphant drumbeat.

Mine. Mine. Thrusting forward, I slide deeper. *Mine.*

And she's so tight where she grips me; so slick and hot and perfect. I've dreamed of this moment so many times, but nothing compares to the reality of this woman.

I sink deeper with a groan.

On and on, I nudge forward. Fliss widens her legs; she gasps against my neck. She's trembling, and so am I.

"This," I grit out between clenched teeth, "is fucking paradise."

Her laugh is muffled against my throat. Sweat trickles between my shoulder blades, and I thrust forward the last few inches, then... I'm in.

We're sealed together, as deep as we can go.

My shaft throbs. I can feel her pulse down there; can feel every flutter of her inner muscles. I swear I can hear her blood rushing through her veins.

"Fliss." I kiss her shoulder, her chin, her eyelids. "Are you alright? Do you want to keep going?"

Ten fingernails dig into my ass. "Don't you dare stop, Bamford. If you come this far then stop, I'll kill you."

No fear.

When I rock forward in a haze, pleasure crackles along my spine. My girl tosses her head and groans.

We're built for each other. Made for this.

The headboard knocks against the wall, and the bed frame creaks. The mattress springs go *plink, plink, plink.*

Sweat trickles into my eyes and I blink it away. Muscles burning, face hot. My lips taste like salt and sweat and *Fliss*—the earthy tang between her legs, where she grips me now. It's everything and it's not enough and I'm thrusting harder, moving faster, trying to claim her from the inside.

"Oooh," she moans, her eyes screwed shut. I kiss her hard, and she sucks on my tongue. Pleasure slices through my gut like a razor blade.

Time stretches out—we've been at this for minutes, and also for eternity. Never want it to end, but if I don't come soon, I'm going to bite through my own tongue.

Jamming a hand between us again, I rub her clit. Stroke the sensitive flesh around her entrance, growling when my fingertips brush my shaft as it plunges in and out of her body. Chasing her higher and higher and *higher*.

Her breath catches. Fliss goes still, muscles rippling, strangling me inside her.

She comes with a strangled squeak.

Thank god.

I follow a minute later, bellowing like a wounded animal, and she'll definitely tease me for that later but I don't care. Can't think about anything except her slick body gripping me, *milking* me, and the primal satisfaction of filling her with long, desperate spurts.

Mine.

I grab a pillow and squeeze it until my knuckles creak. I'm still coming. This can't be natural. She's sucking out my goddamn soul.

And when I collapse on my assistant, her fingertips stroking through my hair, I'm abashed. Breathing hard. "Sorry. That was… a lot."

Fliss hums and wriggles her hips. It's a mess down there, sloshing shamelessly, but when I lift my head, she gives me a sinful smile.

"You'll need to rehydrate, boss. I'm definitely gonna want that again tonight."

Okay, I'm doomed. I'll never make it to morning.

But what a way to go.

* * *

Three years later

Guests mill across the lawn, the scent of roses carried on

the breeze. Everyone is dressed to impress, sipping from champagne flutes and making polite conversation. String music drifts through the evening.

My wife pauses next to a statue of a Greek hero. The stone man is trussed up with string lights, and ivy grows over his plinth.

"You know what?" Fliss says. "Screw this. I should've worn the sandals." She kicks off her heels, bare toes scrunching against the grass.

I pick them up without comment. Every year, it's the same—but I don't mind. We're all creatures of habit in our own way, and I wouldn't change a thing about this woman. Not even if it means carrying her heels around the Bamfords' garden parties every year.

"Oh look, there's your mom and Maude." Fliss sets off and I stroll after her, sipping champagne. It's tart and sweet and bubbly, just like the woman of my dreams.

The breeze tugs at her hair as she strides across the grass. The raspberry streaks are long gone, replaced for the time being by teal-dipped ends. My mother's smile is warm when she sees us, and she fusses over the new hair, arranging the locks over my wife's shoulders.

She loves us both really. Especially Fliss.

It helps that I told her in no uncertain terms three years ago that Fliss and I are a package deal. She could have both of us around, or neither. And once she got to know my girl... well, who could resist Felicity? My mother didn't stand a chance. None of us did.

"Orange juice?" she asks now as I reach them. My mother raises an eyebrow at my wife's glass, hope sparking in her eyes.

"Keep it to yourselves," I say. Fliss leans into my side and I kiss her head. "For now, anyway." Her bump will be obvious soon enough.

My grandmother beams at me, wrinkles shifting around her round face. My mother raises her glass in a toast. "To family. And to your good health, Felicity."

Glasses clink, and I blink up at the sky, eyes prickling. Who ever thought I'd get so lucky?

Fliss is mine, and for the rest of our lives, I get to make her happy. When my relatives turn away, chatting together, I lean down to my wife.

"Screw the small talk. Meet me in the hedge maze in ten minutes."

II

Grump Gone Bad

Description

I've worked for my boss for years without a single spark between us.

Now his twin brother has set me ablaze.

I know as soon as I step into the penthouse office: this man is not my boss. No way. He has the same suit, same hair, same piercing blue eyes, but… nope. I'm not buying it.

Because my boss has never set my pulse racing. Not once. But *this* guy…

One single look and I'm struggling for breath.

He says they've swapped places for a few days. He's filling in for his twin, and I'm to work as normal. Keep up the ruse.

Cool cool cool. Except I'm a terrible liar.

And he's staring like he wants to eat me alive.

Priya

Something's off the second I step into the office.

There are well-dressed people all around, chatting and flirting and stressing about deadlines as they march across the lobby. That's normal enough. The old fashioned cage elevator grinds its way to the top floor with a series of crunches and bangs, and that's damnably normal too.

The Landry & Co offices are sunlit and bustling, with more foliage than a tropical rainforest, and even before 8am the whole building thrums with energy.

Normal. All normal.

But the back of my neck prickles.

Something's off.

Adjusting my grip on a cardboard tray of coffees, I offer the pair of junior architects in the elevator with me a polite smile. They're both fresh out of college, the man wearing a pinstripe suit and sneakers, the woman in a silk t-shirt and blazer. Cool but professional. I'm outclassed in my faded purple sheath dress.

They ignore me, chatting about the big pitch next Friday. Assistants are invisible like that—we only pop into existence when someone needs us. I'll see these jerks later when they want a peek at the boss's schedule.

Numbers flicker past on the little screen. The elevator cranks to a halt on floor eighteen to let out the rude newbies, then I'm alone, juddering into the heavens.

With no one to witness me, I yawn so wide my jaw cracks. My roommate's cat kept me awake last night crying for his mom. She's off on some messed up trip with her boss, fake dating for his family and pretending they don't have real feelings for each other, and I'm left playing cat nanny for the long weekend.

I don't mind really. Rusty's a cute little fuzzball.

But I got *no* sleep last night, and now a headache curdles behind my right eye.

Bang. Crunch. The elevator struggles all the way to the top floor, and I exit on wobbly legs. I've told Mr Landry a million times that the elevator is scary and weird, but he insists that it brings a vintage feel to the building.

Oh, and it's perfectly safe. Definitely an afterthought.

Architects. Honestly.

It's always quieter on the top floor, all the frenetic energy kept below. I stroll through the hushed corridor, past my own neat desk where it stands guard, all the way into the boss's office.

"Coffee," I call like every morning. This way I start the day as a savior; a caffeine-bearing angel. It's worth the two minute detour on my walk here.

Mr Landry glances up behind his desk and nods. "Thank you, Priya." He's wearing his usual Friday suit—charcoal gray with a sage green shirt—and his dark hair is pushed back from his forehead. All normal.

But I slam to a halt, cardboard tray creaking in my grip, my heart suddenly pounding at one hundred miles an hour.

Because even though he looks exactly the same, even though he wears the same clothes and knows my name, that man is *not* my boss. I'd stake my life on it. What the hell is going on?

The man behind the desk notices my freak-out. He tilts his head and smiles, slow and devilish.

I stumble back a step.

* * *

"Well, that lasted," the man makes a show of checking his watch, "less than five seconds. A triumph."

"Wh-who are you?" The coffees wobble in my hand. I should put them down, should spare the *real* Mr Landry's priceless rug, but the nearest flat surface is the boss's desk and you couldn't pay me to step closer to the strange man.

The man who looks like a carbon copy of my boss. Same square jaw, same piercing blue eyes. Did he find a doppelganger somewhere in the city? Or does he have...

"A twin," I mumble, answering my own question. God, I'm slow first thing in the morning. Even though it's rude, I pluck one of the coffees from the tray and swig from it, scalding my tongue.

"Tom never mentioned me?"

I shake my head, still guzzling coffee like my life depends on it. It's hot and sweet and milky, and I need it more than air. The headache flares brighter in my temple.

"I'm filling in for a few days. Keeping up appearances."

79

Who does this? What the hell? What about the huge pitch next week?

"He said that you do eighty percent of his work anyway, and the rest he'll send over email. You should breathe, by the way."

I lower the half-empty coffee cup, wheezing and queasy. I've always known my boss can be a flake—god knows I've made up plenty of excuses on days when he skips meetings to go kite surfing—but this is a new low.

The replacement Mr Landry watches me from behind the desk, pale eyes intense. He's so *still*. With floor-to-ceiling plants behind him, he's like a panther in the foliage.

"No one will buy it," I say, waving a trembling hand at—at *him*. "It's so obvious."

Another flickering smile. "Actually, you're the only person who's ever told us apart. Even our mother can't do it. Isn't that interesting, Priya? How exactly can you tell?"

"It's..." Well. If I'm honest with myself, here's what it is:

The butterflies in my stomach. The way my skin heats when this man looks at me. The way every nerve ending in my body crackled to life when I saw him, an electric current zinging through my veins. It's the way something deep inside me *recognized* him, called out to him, but obviously I can't say any of that.

"Your posture," I say instead, and it sounds so lame. "You sit differently. And you're more still."

"Huh." My fake boss shifts in his chair, the leather creaking. "What if I fidget? Is that more convincing?"

How should I know? It's still painfully obvious to me.

Because I've worked for Tom Landry for three years, and my pulse has never once fluttered in his presence. My mouth has never gone dry at the sight of his hands. But a single glance at his twin brother, and I'm sweating through my dress.

"Excuse me," I rasp, and flee back to my own desk, slamming the office door shut behind me.

I took the second coffee, but I'm not even sorry. I need it way more than he does.

Emmett

This is fascinating. Leaning back in my brother's chair, legs stretched out beneath the desk, I allow myself a grin. The sunshine is warm where it spills through the huge glass windows, and a puff of cloud drifts across the blue sky.

A week, Tom said. A week of stalking around this building and letting myself be seen, and in return he'd owe me a favor and a bottle of fine whiskey. And I've done this plenty of times before—passed myself off as Tom and tried not to die of boredom—but it's never thrilled me like this.

She could tell. Immediately, as soon as Priya stepped into the room, she could tell.

How? What's so special about Tom's assistant?

Sure, she spends hours with him in this building every week, but our own family members can't tell us apart. Nor our teachers at school, or our friends and girlfriends back in college. *That* made for a few awkward encounters, let me tell you.

"Priya Dhawan." I say her name slowly, rolling it around

my tongue like I could taste it. Tom mentioned her, of course, but he didn't give many details. Didn't mention her wide-eyed beauty, or the way her husky voice makes every sentence sound like pillow talk. Did he leave that out on purpose? Trying to throw me off the trail?

Maybe they're together. He wouldn't be the first boss to sleep with an assistant, and surely not the last. I push to my feet, grin fading.

The puff of cloud drifts in front of the sun, dimming the morning sky for one heartbeat. I push through the door.

Priya's at her desk, her knee jiggling under the table. Her silky dark hair is tied in a high ponytail, the ends dancing as she vibrates with tension. How many coffees has she had this morning? All that caffeine, then this shock... I round the desk and peer into her dazed face.

Smooth tawny skin and a flush on her cheeks. Thick, arching eyebrows over brown, soulful eyes.

Beautiful.

And I signed up for a standard-regulation twin swap: no harm done. I will not be responsible for this young woman's heart attack.

A few steps to the water cooler. There's a gurgling rush of bubbles; an interminable wait. I return and place the cup by her hand, saying, "Drink this, please."

Priya huffs, staring past me down the corridor, but she takes the cup. It wobbles on its path to her mouth—lips pursed and painted a dark red color that would stain my shirt collar in the best way.

Her throat works as she swallows. The cup taps against the wooden desk, empty after three gulps. "Where is Mr Landry?"

I am also Mr Landry, but fine. "Tom's upstate."

"Why—?"

"Personal reasons." I wince, remembering my suspicion from a moment ago, because if Priya and Tom are sleeping together, she will not like why he's gone. "Does it matter?"

Are you together? That's what I really want to know. It started as idle curiosity, but the longer I stare at this woman, the more the question needles my insides. She's too good for him, surely. Too regal, too smart. Even now, in the midst of this shock, her shoulders are back and she regards me with steady calm.

My twin brother is a lot of things, but a decent boyfriend is not one of them. Never has been. It's a sore spot between us; the cause of several fights back in college, punches thrown on the quad for honor's sake. And *this* woman...

Well, she's a winning lottery ticket. I've only known her for a few minutes, and even I see that. He'd better not mess her around, or I swear to god, I'll toss him around this office. Don't care if we're years too old for that shit.

"You're angry," Priya observes, folding her hands on the desk. Her fingernails are short and neat, painted indigo blue. "Why?"

Because my brother's an asshole, and she apparently knows him better than our own relatives. Surely they're sleeping together.

The thought spreads through my insides like acid, eating away at my organs and bones. What is wrong with me? Why do I care?

"Maybe I'm tired of foolish questions." Inhaling sharply, I rub my chest. What is that slicing pain? "It's Emmett, by the way. Since you didn't ask."

"Charmed," Priya says, her voice so flat, and Christ, I'm messing this up in the worst way. Blaming the one innocent person in this scenario; lashing out like a wounded animal because there's a slim chance my brother has seen her naked.

So what if he has? It's none of my business.

Fuck.

"I'll keep out of your way." It's harder than it should be to walk back to the office doorway—like wading through water. "Tom's got his cell if you have a work-related question. Don't bother him otherwise."

Her irritated scoff follows me into the office. I close the door, then lean against it with my palms pressed flat. Guilt and shame squeeze my throat.

What the hell have I gotten myself into? A week with that woman? With her reproachful glances and her disappointed sighs?

Sounds like purgatory. I fish my phone out of my pocket with a shaking hand, but Tom's dial tone is busy. Figures. Guess I'm not the only one ready to curse him out.

Closing my eyes, I wait for my heartbeats to slow. Priya's faint voice drifts through the door, hardening each time she says my name.

* * *

When I finally get through to Tom on the desk phone, he's already laughing. "Dude," he says, like he's still a college student and not a CEO in his late thirties, "Priya busted you so hard. I wish I could've seen your face. It's Jenna McCay all over again."

Jenna was Tom's steady girlfriend in the first year of college. He made me go on a date with her in his place for one night— a few hours at the cinema—and I spent the whole evening wracked with guilt, desperately trying to keep ten inches of space between us at all times. I confessed as soon as the movie ended and we spilled out into the night air, and Jenna slapped me so hard that her hand print glowed on my cheek.

Who could blame her? That was not a proud moment for me. My idiot nineteen year old self deserved that slap, just like Tom deserved Jenna dumping him like old leftovers. She could do far better.

"It's nothing like Jenna McCay." I tug on the collar of Tom's shirt, grimacing at the abstract painting on his office wall. How can he stand these monkey suits? I can't breathe. "We agreed back then: no more personal situations. And you and Priya aren't personally involved."

I wait, heart pounding, desperate for his confirmation, but Tom doesn't take the bait. He says, "Priya's scary when she's mad, isn't she?"

No. Not really. The young woman out there is dignified— poised when everyone around her is behaving like a jackass. But I can see why Tom finds that unsettling.

Still, I won't hear it. "Don't talk shit about Priya."

He splutters. "I'm not! She's the best assistant I've ever had." And..? *And..?*

I swear to god, if I don't get a straight answer soon, I'm going to gnaw through the wood of Tom's fancy desk. "Are you sleeping with her?"

Screw it. I need to know.

He laughs again, loud and bright, like it's the funniest thing he's ever heard. I sink back in the chair, my pulse finally slowing, and stop tugging on my collar. Tom sure doesn't sound like a man who just got rumbled.

Thank god.

"No," my brother says at last, "I am not sleeping with Priya. For one thing, she's my assistant, and for another, she's not my type."

Not his type? That makes no sense. Beautiful and resilient and smart aren't his type? With this fresh insight into my brother's taste, I respect him a little less... even as I'm glad for it.

The phone crackles as he changes ear. "She's not into us either."

Us? "What do you mean?"

"She's never looked at me twice. And I hate to break this to you, Emmett, but we have the same face."

The same eminently slappable face.

Right.

"Keep your hands off my assistant," Tom says, mock-stern. "It's the weekend tomorrow, then only a few days more. Just... hide in the office and do DIY or whatever. Let her run the show, she's more than capable."

My fingers itch for my tool kit. Now that he's suggested it, it's all I want. "You got anything up here that needs fixing?"

"The faucet leaks in my bathroom. And one of the lights in the corridor flickers. Hold up, I'll send you a list."

Yeah. Okay. Fixing things for a few days—I can do that. Sounds almost calming.

And I can keep my hands off Priya Dhawan for a week.

Definitely.

Priya

꞉꞉꞉

"You're tense." My roommate Maisie comes to stand behind the sofa, prodding at my bunched-up shoulders. "These muscles are rock hard."

Rusty purrs on my lap, drooling on my pajama pants. It's a Sunday morning, and the two of us are watching cartoons until his mom comes home. Our other roommate, Fliss, should be back today, and then I'm off cat duty.

I'm trying not to be sad about that.

Because I know Rusty's not my pet, but I *need* him right now. My work life has turned upside down, and I'm wrestling with the world's most unwelcome crush. Rusty's my only comfort.

"Want a back rub?"

Maisie's a massage therapist. And not just any massage therapist—the owner of the most sought-after healing hands in the city. She has this magic aura, this incredible sense of calm, and it's no wonder that her schedule books out months in advance. Even chatting with her for a few minutes lowers my blood pressure.

"That would be amazing. Are you sure you don't mind?"

It's her job, after all. She's off duty. The last thing I'd want to do with *my* weekend is file reports and send emails, especially when my boss is such a grade A jerk.

But Maisie's a sweetheart. A black-haired, freckle-faced sweetheart. "Shuffle up," she says.

Rusty squeaks as I wriggle along the sofa, his claws gripping my thighs. I turn my back to my roommate and she settles behind me, the sofa cushions sinking under our shared weight.

Cartoons flicker on the TV, the volume low. The morning sunshine spills golden through the window.

"We should clean before Fliss comes back," I say.

Maisie hums, her small hands gliding over my shoulders. "Don't worry about that right now. You're always so *on*, Priya."

Is that a bad thing? It's how I'm so good at my job; how I got high grades in school. How I keep the vast, swirling chaos of the universe at bay.

Piercing blue eyes drift through my mind, and I suppress a shiver. Guess some things can't be controlled after all.

And... what is Emmett Landry doing right now? Is he still pretending to be his brother? Or will he be himself again over the weekend?

"My boss switched places with his twin brother." The words blurt out of me, barely louder than the TV. And I know I promised discretion, but god, if I don't tell somebody I'll explode.

Plus Maisie would never spill the beans, not even about something as wild as this. There's a massage therapist code of silence, or something.

"There was a different Mr Landry at the office on Friday. He'll be there next week too. No one else can tell them apart, but I can."

Maisie's quiet for a long moment, her thumbs digging into a knot by my shoulder blade. Then: "Wow. That's nuts. Okay, I see now why you're all scrunchy."

"Right?" A long breath gusts out of me, and honestly, hearing Maisie say that is almost as relaxing as the massage. I'm not overreacting. This *is* bananas. "His name's Emmett. He spent the whole day on Friday banging around tools in the boss's office. I think maybe he's a builder."

That would explain his broad shoulders and those scarred hands. The more I think about it, the more I see the differences between the two men. Is everyone else blind?

For example: my boss has a strict gym regimen and the toned, deliberate muscles to prove it. He also gets secret manicures once a month. I know, because I book them.

Whereas Emmett has that brawny, organic strength that comes from moving a bunch of heavy stuff, day in, day out, and calluses on his hands. Maybe he's less magazine-worthy, a bit rougher around the edges, but it sure gets *me* all hot and bothered.

"You just tensed up again. What are you thinking?" Maisie kneads my shoulders, and I melt again under her magic hands. With my fingers playing through Rusty's fur, we've got a cute little massage train here.

"Okay... don't judge me."

"Never." Her reply is quick and sure, and that's why I love this girl. "I know you, Priya. You can tell me anything."

My mouth twists, and I tickle Rusty's brown belly. He bats at my wrist, but those claws stay sheathed. Such a gentle, sticky little angel.

"I've never... had a crush like this."

Maisie works a knot between my ribs. "On your boss?"

"No, on his brother. The imposter." And saying it out loud is so ridiculous, so humiliating, that I rush to fill Maisie's thoughtful silence. "I know it's nothing. But it's like I'm hyper-attuned to his presence. We only spent one day near each other, but my ears were straining for his every move through the walls. And whenever he came into the room, my skin prickled, and I could barely sit still. Obviously it's pheromones or something. And one-sided. And a terrible idea. And if anything happened and then someone caught us, they'd think I was messing around with my boss. And if my *real* boss found out, he'd freak out and fire me. And Emmett barely spoke to me anyway, and when he did he was a jerk, so it doesn't matter."

"Hmm," Maisie says. "Hmm."

Rusty gnaws on my thumb knuckle without biting down. His breath smells like fish.

"Did he seem interested in you too?" she asks.

My mouth twists as I consider that question. Did my fake boss seem unsettled by me at all? He certainly found plenty of excuses to come and visit me at my desk, never mind our rough start. And when I took his lunch through at midday, he lit up like a sunrise.

But that could be, you know. His standard reaction to a free sandwich.

"I'm not sure," I hedge. "Maybe?"

Hopefully.

"You don't have many crushes," my roommate says at last. Her hands are warm on my back through my pajama shirt, and I gaze out of the sunny window, eyes unfocused. Ivy climbs the brick building opposite, all fuzzy and green in my haze.

"Nope," I say. Try never. This is new territory for me.

91

I've never laid awake at night before like I have this weekend, one man's wicked smile fixed in my brain. I've never tossed and turned and whimpered under my breath, desperate for those specific calloused hands to run all over my bare body.

I've never longed to hear a deep, gravelly voice say my name one more time, the ache splitting open my chest.

Clearly, I've lost my mind. I don't even know the man. Not really.

Even if it feels like, on some soul-deep level, I do.

"These feelings are garbage." I rub the line of Rusty's nose. "How do people stand it?"

"I wouldn't know," Maisie says, soft and amused. "But when I find my own world-ending crush, I'll give you an answer."

"Well, hurry up," I grumble. "I'm dying here."

Even her laugh is soothing. "It'll be okay, Priya. It's only a few more days, and then you'll probably never have to see this man again."

Was that supposed to make me feel better? Because it really, really doesn't.

* * *

Monday morning brings the sharp tang of fresh paint. I wander into Mr Landry's office, coffee tray gripped in one hand, and my mouth drops open.

It's... a building site. Literally. Dust sheets cover the furniture; a paint-splattered step ladder stands by the window. A tangle of wires dangles down where a light fitting used to be, and Mr Landry's priceless rug is rolled up by the wall.

"Oh my god." My hand sweats around my satchel strap. The coffees wobble in my hand. "What have you done?"

Emmett glances at me over his shoulder. He's inspecting the green wall of foliage behind the boss's desk. "Are these plants delicate?" he asks. "Will they die if I take them down for a few hours?"

How the hell should I know? I'm an assistant, not a freaking gardener—and clearly my expression tells him so, because Emmett shrugs and turns back to the plants. His strong fingers delve through the leaves, inspecting the metal frame they're fixed to.

"Don't take them down," I grit out when I find my voice again. "Mr Landry loves that wall. He says it's his calling card. He's been pushing this green design initiative, because he says it's the future, and Mr Landry—"

"Perhaps you should call him Tom." My fake boss's voice is sour. He addresses the leaves. "To save confusion."

Seriously? "It's not that complicated. Mr Landry is my boss, and *you*," I gesture around the ruined office with the coffee tray, "are the man giving me an ulcer." Partly for work reasons, and partly... not. It's not only anger heating my cheeks. Somehow, in between all the sex dreams, I forgot how striking he is. "You know he'll blame me for this, right? I'm supposed to keep everything in order."

"He won't blame you," Emmett says, stepping back and folding his arms. When he glances at me over his shoulder again, I'm hit with the shock of those ice blue eyes. "Tom knows I can't sit on my hands for a week. If he wants me to take his place, I need a project while I'm here."

God. I press my knuckles against my temple. "If anyone comes up here looking for the boss and sees you like this—"

"Like what?" Emmett grins. "Oh, you mean this?" Strong fingers pluck at his gray t-shirt, splattered with dozens of paint colors. Long gone are Friday's pinstripes, replaced with old cotton and faded jeans. "Don't worry, I've got Tom's precious suit in the en suite. I need it for some bullshit video conference later. If anyone comes looking, you stall them and I'll change."

"That won't explain your office! And where are you going to sit for that conference? This room is a wreck!"

Emmett smiles wider. "We'll figure it out."

Oh my god. He's enjoying this, isn't he? Relishing the chaos he's created. This man is my exact opposite in every way.

Because I'm a rule follower. A good girl. I never miss a deadline, and I always arrive ten minutes early for my appointments. I walk the same route to work, use the same laundry detergent, and watch the same TV shows, day in and day out.

This man is a controlled explosion. He's a detonation on legs.

Long, muscled legs that look great in paint-splattered jeans. Gah.

"Just... promise me you can fix everything. You'll put it back as it was."

Emmett turns on his heel and strides over, his big body suddenly filling my vision. Warm palms land on my shoulders, kneading the muscles there, and the coffee tray trembles between us. Gosh, he's tall.

"I promise," he says, those blue eyes so close, "that I will fix everything. And though it won't look exactly the same, it will be a million times better. I won't let you get in trouble for this, okay? Trust me, Priya."

And I've lost it. Because... I do trust him. I do. And with those hands on me, with that steady, fond smile like he's known me for years, the tightness in my chest loosens. My lungs work again, drawing down gulps of paint-scented air.

Did he think about me over the weekend at all?

That's a crazy thing to wonder—and now he's watching me patiently, waiting for a response.

I nod, biting my lip.

Emmett's gaze flicks down. "Is that second coffee for me?"

"You don't deserve it." The cup scrapes against the cardboard tray, and I hand it over. His fingers brush mine as the cup changes hands. "Be careful, it's hot."

"Yes, ma'am."

When I stumble back a step, I'm so flustered. What was I doing when I came up here? What's on my To Do list for today? I can't think straight. My brain's too full with Emmett Landry and the smattering of dark chest hairs peeking above his stretched-out t-shirt neckline. The fabric looks soft, brushing against the planes of his chest.

Does that hair trail down his belly? Why do I like that thought so much?

And why oh why did my body save its big sexual awakening for this man? So unfair.

"Um. I'll send around an email saying you're in meetings all day and that you don't want to be disturbed."

"Sounds good."

"And I guess I'll order your lunch later?"

Emmett's smile is crooked. "Fancy. Thanks, Priya."

My cheeks are on fire as I hightail it out of there. He's my boss's *brother*, damn it.

One thing is for sure: this will not end well.

Emmett

"We can't keep pulling this shit." It's Tuesday evening, the sky tinged lilac as the sun sets, and I'm walking home along the river path. My shoulders strain against another of Tom's tailored suits, and his pair of buffed leather brogues creak with every step. They rub my heels, and the soles are thinner than sheet metal.

It felt awful shucking my painting gear and putting on Tom's clothes before leaving the office. Like putting on a straitjacket. How can he bear it?

Tom sighs in my ear, static crackling through the phone, and it's so familiar. I'm more acquainted with my brother's noises than my own.

"It's not a big deal. We've been swapping places our whole lives, Em."

Exactly. Not often, especially the last decade, but often enough. When does it end?

Besides—it's always me filling in for Tom, never the other way around. Me sitting in his college classes, taking notes; me visiting our mom twice in one day when she was sick last year, wearing different clothes each time so the heartbreak of an absent son wouldn't make her feel any worse. I wasn't proud of that lie, but at least she lit up at Tom's 'visit'.

I'm tired of cleaning up my brother's messes. Tired of giving into his appeals so easily, always ready to take the fall. I'm eight minutes older, but sometimes it feels more like eight years.

I'm the one who has the hard conversations. The one who weathers the public judgment when Tom goes astray. And I'm sick of it. I'm too old for this shit.

"People will notice eventually. Priya won't be the only one who knows."

Tom's voice hardens. "Why do you say that? Did she threaten to tell someone?"

Ducks flap across the water, quacking and splashing, and I slam to a halt, the heel of one palm digging into my forehead. My head aches like hell. And lord knows I'm not an angry man in general—I'm quicker to laugh than to yell—but if my brother was standing in front of me right now, I might wring his useless neck.

How dare he talk like that? Like *Priya* is the problem? Like she's a bug to be squashed?

She's the only noble one out of all three of us. How did this asshole ever build an architecture firm?

"This has nothing to do with Priya," I say, my throat tight. "She's been discreet. Helpful, even." In truth, she's been the only bright spot in this whole mess, her presence a reward I don't deserve. "I'm talking about the fact that I'm a grown man and I'm playing dress up in my brother's clothes."

A snort. "Well, at least it's an improvement. You could hardly run Landry & Co in your ancient flannel."

97

"*Tom.*" He's not listening. He never listens to things he doesn't want to hear, but I want it on the record anyway. "This is the last time, okay? Don't ask me again, because I'll say no. I shouldn't have agreed this time. I only said yes because of... you know."

There's a beat of silence. I start walking again, little stones crunching beneath my feet. Long, thick reeds cling to the riverbank, and unknown critters rustle in them as I pass. Insects buzz as the red sun sinks lower.

It's a warm night. Where does Priya live? Does she change when she gets home? What are her comfy clothes like? She seems so professional at work, so buttoned-up.

I'd love to see her laze around in sweats, hair up and face bare of makeup. Preferably no bra, but that's my inner pervert talking.

"I'm sorry, Em." My brother is quieter now. Chastened. "I know I shouldn't have asked. You've got your own life, your own business, and I've got no right to expect this of you."

My steps slow. I'm less agitated, strolling again, listening to my brother dredge up the words he owes.

"I'll give Priya a raise when I'm back," he says, and that's more like it. "Some kind of promotion, too. It's long overdue anyway."

"Good." I feel lighter already. This has been a worthwhile call. "You do that, Tom."

"And I'll visit Mom. I'll get my shit together. It's just—it's been a weird few weeks, you know?"

Yeah, I get it. Because I know where Tom is right now, while I'm pretending to be him in the run-up to his firm's big bid. I know only the most major revelation could drag him away at such a crucial time. He loves Landry & Co, and when he's passionate about something, he doesn't flake. Not when it counts.

"How's the baby?" The secret baby, born to a mother he hooked up with one time and forgot. The son he didn't realize he was about to have until a few days ago. Every time I think about my surprise nephew, I thank my lucky stars that I've never sowed my wild oats like my brother has. They called him Tom Cat in college for a reason.

"Squishy," he says. "I'll send you a picture."

"Please."

A cool breeze ruffles the reeds and sends ripples across the water. My footsteps echo.

"Thank god there's only one of him," Tom says.

I shudder, thinking of all the ways we were demons as kids. Clattering around and screaming, always playing pranks on our mom. "Tell me about it."

"It makes you think, you know? I've been wondering a lot over the last few days, trying to figure out what I've been doing with my life and why."

"Yeah." Surprise progeny will do that to a man, or so I'd imagine. "Just... take care of the baby. Take care of the mother. Everything else will fall into place."

Tom hums, and he sounds so melancholy and tired. Like a man who's felt the world rock under his feet. "Damn, Emmett. When did you get so wise?"

"In the eight minutes before you turned up." Tom laughs, and my heart aches in answer. This man has been my closest companion through life, even when he's driven me up the wall, and now a little mite has come along to take my place as number one. It's ridiculous of me, but I'm already lonely.

Well, Tom had better do right by them, or he'll have me to

answer to.

"Be good to them, Tom Cat."

"I will."

* * *

The next morning, Priya finds me in a philosophical mood, arms folded over my chest as I stare out of Tom's office window. It's one of those days where the weather can't make its mind up, sunny one moment, spitting with rain the next. Shafts of sunlight spear through dark clouds.

I glower at the rooftops, and I guess this is why some people call me a grump. I'm not a yeller, but I've got resting grouch face.

"Wow," Priya says, bringing our morning coffees. She zig-zags a careful path through the dust sheets, tools and tins of paint. Tendrils of steam curl from the coffee lids. "Now you look like Mr Landry. That's the exact look he gets after talking with the city planners."

It's hard to imagine Tom being serious at work. He so rarely is with me. But how else would he build a successful company? We all contain different versions of ourselves, I guess.

And I'm not sure which version of me is driving right now, but all I know is I can't stay in these four walls. I'm gonna crawl out of my skin. "Hey," I say as Priya gets close. "Want to get out of here?"

Her eyebrows raise as she passes me my coffee. Our fingers brush, like every morning—like we have a tacit agreement to touch. Warmth tickles over my skin.

"Where would we go?" she asks.

It's my first smile of the morning. My cheeks feel stiff.

"There's a whole, wide world out there, Priya."

"Don't be an ass." She purses her lips and blows through the hole in her coffee lid. That lipstick. God. "Where exactly do you want to go?"

With her? Anywhere. I could sit in a ditch at the side of a highway with this woman and call it a good time. But she's right, I do have somewhere in mind.

Because even if it's only for a few stolen days, I want her to know me. The real Emmett—not the one in Tom's office, in Tom's clothes. We don't have much time left together.

"I could show you what I'm working on. In my *real* job, as Emmett Landry. I think you might like it," I add, and fuck, I'm babbling. Why am I nervous right now? I feel like I'm asking Priya to the world's lamest prom.

It's a casual offer. It doesn't matter if she says no. But when Priya smiles, her eyes crinkling, and nods her agreement, I soar up to the clouds in relief.

"Alright. Put the next person in the food chain in charge, then meet me in the lobby. Act normal."

She snorts, and when she shakes her head, the sunshine shimmers against her dark brown hair. "*You* act normal. Mr Landry never grins like that, Emmett. You'll give us away."

"No chance." I sip my coffee, and sweet, milky warmth spreads over my tongue. "No one sees me but you, sweetheart."

Priya

I've never once played hooky in my whole life. Why would I? I'm a goody-two-shoes; Prim Priya with her flawless record and her boring, lonely life.

Not anymore. Not with Emmett here to turn me bad. I'm fizzing with excitement as we march down the street, his strides twice as long as mine, our shoes splashing through shallow puddles.

Who cares about the bid on Friday? That's for the architects to worry about. My whole job is to assist a man who's not here.

"Where's your car?"

Emmett said we'd drive out of the city.

"Truck. And it's parked at my place. You don't mind a twenty minute walk, do you?"

Nope, I do not. Not even when the clouds rumble overhead, static crackling in the air, threatening more rain, and especially not once Emmett slows his pace to match mine.

We wander along the river path, chatting about everything and nothing, pointing at the ducks, and he slings his suit jacket over his shoulder. Tugs the top buttons of his shirt free.

It's almost funny how much this man hates office wear. He's so out of place in his brother's life. How can no one else see it?

"Are you a builder?"

Emmett shrugs, jacket dancing. "Meh. Sort of."

"A house flipper?"

His slow smile makes me so gooey. Hot and flustered and aching for something mysterious. "You're getting warmer."

"Are you—"

"I'll show you, Priya," he says, cutting me off. "Patience, young one."

I'm not *that* young. There must be less than a decade between us. Probably.

Two ducks have a blazing row on the river as we walk past, lunging at each other and quacking. Spots of water glint in the air, and a rope of pond weed splatters against the bank. I brush my fingertips along the reeds, pressing them like piano keys.

When was the last time I felt relaxed like this? *Truly* relaxed, not put in a stupor by Maisie's magic hands?

I don't remember. All I know is I feel more awake today than I have in months—and yet my muscles are loose, my heartbeat calm. The air smells like damp soil and muddy water.

"I wish you were my real boss."

Emmett frowns at the path ahead, and oh god, I've said the wrong thing. My stomach sinks. Is he annoyed on behalf of his brother?

But all he says is, "You won't think that when you see my work."

Doubtful. I'd take any excuse to spend all day with this man. I'd even empty his trash cans and sweep floors, and I hate cleaning.

But I don't say any of that out loud. There's a new tension between us now, and I don't like it. Can't figure it out, even though I put it there.

My mouth twists as I stare out at the birds.

* * *

Emmett's truck is big, blue and rumbling, with an empty flatbed and a single leather bench as the front seat. I cling to the handle above the passenger door, trying not to slide into his lap as we round endless sharp bends, climbing our way into the mountains.

We're less than an hour out of the city, the urban sprawl still visible where it's sandwiched between the mountains and coast, but already this feels like another world.

The air is pine fresh. The sun's hotter, the wind cold. And Emmett Landry, the man who teased me only this morning, is solemn as he drives the mountain path, chest and arms bulging in his twin brother's shirt.

I stare at his scarred knuckles where they clench the steering wheel, my eyes dry. Where did I go wrong? How did I ruin everything already?

"This is it." It's been so long since we spoke, Emmett's low voice makes me jump. He steers off the path onto a driveway, half hidden among the mossy rocks and trees, and my clammy hand clings harder to the handle as we bounce along a dirt road.

As I watch, Emmett gives a little shake; he shucks his bad mood like his twin brother's tailored jacket. And when he glances at me, he's smiling again. "You ready, Priya?"

"...Yeah." Ready to make some sense of this man. Talk about a weather vane.

The house is hard to spot at first, camouflaged between trees. I lean forward, the leather bench squeaking against my thighs, and squint at shafts of sunlight streaking across pale stone. We trundle closer.

There's a high, arching doorway. Stained glass windows and planters spilling over with flowers. Ivy wraps around the building like a sweater, the house stretching high into the trees, and it's like a secret temple tucked away in the mountainside.

"What on earth?"

Emmett grins properly now, guiding the truck easily over rough patches in the path. He pulls up before the house's stately wooden deck and kills the engine, the truck ticking as it cools.

"It was a chapel back in the day." Called it. "Then a boutique B&B for a while, then a family home. Then it fell into disrepair, and no one's lived here for decades."

No kidding. I can't imagine anyone backing their family car down that rocky path, setting out for soccer practice. But with a little TLC...

"It's pretty isolated out here."

Emmett shrugs, unclipping his seat belt. "It's peaceful, sure. But there's a town a mile or so away. Come on, we'll walk around the outside."

Small twigs and fallen leaves crunch beneath our feet. One sticks to Emmett's borrowed fancy brogues, and he shakes it off, cursing quietly.

Oh, yeah. This guy's at home in heavy work boots and worn jeans, not these suits. Fanning my cheeks, I peer up at the building as we walk a lap, dragging in greedy lungfuls of crisp mountain air.

Now that we're closer, the signs of neglect are clear. The cracks in the pale stone, colonized with moss and ivy; the missing roof tiles high above. Holes in the deck and a few windows boarded over.

"So you flip old houses?"

"I restore them," Emmett says, shoulders loose as we stroll through the trees. The trunks crowd around the house, but it's not threatening. More like they're keeping company. Like Emmett said, it's peaceful. "Sometimes to buy and sell. Sometimes hired by a property owner. The point is the restoration—for me, anyway."

Birds chatter overhead. There's a flurry of wings; the soft thump of a berry dropped on the ground.

Imagine living in a place like this. No wonder they built a chapel here once upon a time—with the sun slanting through the branches, it feels holy.

"So your brother builds new things, and you restore the old."

Emmett puffs out a laugh. "Guess so. Never thought about it that way. Seems like even when I'm trying to do my own thing, I'm still a twin."

And he sounds almost mournful, so that's my excuse for why my hand slips into his, our fingers knotting together. My insides quiver at my own daring, but Emmett is calm as he holds my hand, like it's the most natural thing in the world. "I didn't mean it like that. This has nothing to do with your brother."

"*The* Mr Landry."

"The one and only," I agree. I could never call this man something so stuffy.

A shoulder nudge. "Then who am I, sweetheart?"

"You're Emmett." My cheeks are burning, my throat tight.

Our words are light, casual, but it feels like I'm confessing something. "Simple as that. You don't need to be anyone else."

He hums, squeezing my fingers. "I like that."

So do I. I love everything about this day trip—our stolen hours together, tucked away in the mountains.

I wish it could never end.

Inside, it smells like sawdust and old stone. It's cool in the shadows, but baking hot where the sun shines through stained glass, spilling across the floor like tossed jewels. Emmett leads me carefully across the floorboards, pointing out where it's safe to walk, and he clings tightly enough to my hand that even if I did fall through the floor, I'd dangle like a kite on a string.

"It's beautiful," I say.

Emmett rubs my knuckles with his thumb. "You don't have to whisper," he says, speaking louder than me. "It hasn't been a chapel for a long time."

I chew on my bottom lip, gazing around as we troop through empty rooms and past tree-filled windows. He's right. It's not a chapel now—it's an empty shell. A home waiting to be fixed up by Emmett's capable hands, then filled with laughter and music and cooking smells, some lucky family making it their own.

Eventually, I can't hold it in. I throw up my spare hand, then let it smack against my thigh. "Okay, I'll say it. This is my dream house."

Emmett stills, and peers at me closely. "Oh? Is that true?" His pale blue eyes hold me transfixed, and I gulp. We're standing so near to each other, still holding hands.

"Yeah." I sound strangled, but only because he's gazing at me like that. Warming me down to my toes. "I mean... the trees, the mountains, the history here... what's not to love?"

"But wouldn't you miss the city?"

I half shrug. "Maybe. But you said there's a town close by, right? And anyway, I spend most of my free time in the city parks anyway."

Of course, I'd have to work remotely. Or find a new job. But would that really be such a loss?

Wait, why am I thinking about this so seriously? I could never, ever afford a place like this. It's vision board material, not an actual plan.

"You'll have to send me pictures when it's done," I say, peering up at the high ceiling with its wrought iron chandelier. "Before you sell it."

Emmett grunts and lets go of my hand. He plunges both hands through his hair, wandering away a few steps before turning back to me.

Ice blue eyes pin me in place.

It's the way he's looked at me in my dreams every night. The way he's stared at me over and over in the office the last few days, hungry and contemplative, like he knows he should look away but he can't. Like he feels the same inexplicable draw that I do.

We should avoid each other. It's the smart thing to do.

We don't.

We won't.

But it's a few days together. That's all we need to get through. A few days of playing pretend, acting like he's the real Mr Landry, like we're boss and assistant, and he's not the man who's tailor-made to make my body hum.

Seriously. What *is* it about him? Why do my insides melt as soon as Emmett glances in my direction? Why do my cheeks burn, and my hands shake, and my breaths get quick and shallow whenever he's near?

It's not fear. I've never trusted a man more, even though we've barely met.

No, it's far more troubling than that. I can barely let myself think it.

Unfortunately, Emmett is not nearly so shy.

"Those are your come-hither eyes." His smile is rueful, then it drops away. He draws in a deep, shuddering breath, chest lifting, and when he exhales and frowns at the wall, he looks lost.

Come-hither eyes? Am I really that obvious? I'm not *trying* to send out signals here, I just...

I want him.

So badly.

Would it be so wrong?

"Fuck," Emmett mutters, pinching the bridge of his nose. He shakes his head and turns away, striding across the empty room, then wheels right back around, expression raw.

I go still, trembling with anticipation for whatever he'll do next—like he really is a panther and I'm a giddy little rabbit who'll let him pounce.

"Tell me something, Priya." Emmett sounds pissed, and my pulse spikes. Oh god, what's wrong? "Do you ever look at my brother like that?" He waves a hand at my parted lips; the blush staining my cheeks. My stupid come-hither eyes.

I swallow, heart hammering. Why is he mad? The answer is obvious. "No, I don't."

But he doesn't look convinced, and now it's my turn to bristle. Does he think I'm lying?

"No," I say again, "I don't look at your brother like this. Thanks so much for noticing," I add, voice sour.

Just what every girl wants. For her crush to point out that she's a giant, blushing mess for him, and somehow to be mad about it. Where's the dignity, you know?

"We have the same face," Emmett says, folding his arms like that's such a 'gotcha' moment. Ass.

"Oh, yeah." My hands ball into fists. "And that's all that matters, right? The shape of your nose and the color of your eyes. Never mind about the way you think, or speak, or act. Us girls just want a pretty-looking poster to make out with—character's got nothing to do with it. Jerk," I add under my breath, and it's a weak final word, but it's all I've got.

But Emmett walks closer as I speak, the irritation draining from his face at record speed, and when he stops in front of me, he has the cheek to look pleased. He leans in. "Who said anything about making out, Priya?"

My teeth grind together. He grins.

And when he cups my face, I could howl with relief—or wring his neck. I grip two fistfuls of his borrowed shirt instead, and yank him down another inch to speed things along. "I don't want your freaking twin. Get it in your head."

"Yes, ma'am."

And he's a jerk, such a jerk, but when his mouth meets mine, his kiss is searing hot. It leaves no room for doubt, no more room for bad feelings. I suck in a shaky breath, my eyes fluttering closed.

Finally.

And… *Emmett.* That's what I'm left with in the darkness of my closed eyelids: his name thumping through my veins with every heartbeat; his taste on my tongue. The warmth of his body, and the hard planes of his muscles under my hands, and his soft groans of approval as he kisses me, on and on and on.

110

His hands are in my hair then on my back, pressing us closer. His tongue is in my mouth, and we're sharing breaths, nipping with teeth, hearts beating in time.

Is this what it's like for everyone? Kissing your crush? I'm molten.

There's an invisible hook low in my belly, twisting tighter and tighter—and when I shift my weight, I'm so slick and swollen between my legs, I don't recognize my own body.

I whimper. Want him so badly.

Emmett breaks away. "Is this okay?" He breathes the question against my neck, a fistful of my hair clenched in one hand. His lips trail over my pulse point, and I forget to answer until he gives me a tiny shake. "Priya. Do you like this?"

My hands seek out his shoulders and cling on for balance. My brain has stalled like a learner driver at a stoplight. "Uh. Yeah. I—yes. Keep going."

Emmett curses quietly, relief clear in his voice, then seals his mouth against mine. Once again, everything is right with the universe.

We kiss for a long time. Until our bodies get creaky from standing; until my throat is dry. Until the sun tracks across the midday sky.

When we finally break apart, I'm a brand new person. Reborn in his arms.

"Holy shit," Emmett says.

I'd have to agree.

Emmett

This is a delicate situation, and that calls for tact. Subtlety. Not traits I'm known for.

All I really know is: when I buckle Priya into my truck, ignoring her complaints about how she can do it herself, I'm protecting someone precious. The most precious of all.

And... I've changed. In the space of a few hours, I'm a new man.

It's unsettling. As I slide behind the steering wheel, truck dipping under my weight, I'm not sure I like it.

Because I've always been my own person. As a twin, I fought damn hard for that status—took care to build my own life, my own skill set, my own hopes and dreams, *without* my brother's input. It didn't happen overnight. Would've been easier than breathing to stay latched onto Tom, just like when we were boys, but I didn't want that.

I wanted to fly solo.

Now here I am, chest cracked open and aching, driving in silence back down the mountain path as I try to think of ways

112

to keep this woman beyond the few days we have left. Ways I could mingle our lives together; ways to keep her close. The exact opposite of solo.

It's alien—and so goddamn vulnerable. How do people stand it?

"It's only 3pm," Priya says, and she sounds as dazed as I feel. How can the earth have moved like that, and it's only 3pm? "Can we go back to Landry & Co? I want to check on things for Friday's bid."

"Sure."

I mean, what else am I gonna do with her for the rest of the afternoon? Take her back to my apartment and bury my face between her thighs? Book us flights to Vegas for a quickie wedding? Sounds good, actually.

I'd do it, by the way. I'm all in. Both options work for me, though Priya doesn't seem like a drive-thru nuptials kinda girl.

"We'll have to act normal in the office." It's like she's giving herself a pep talk and I'm eavesdropping. Slender fingers twist together in her lap, and Priya's given up on clutching the handle by the passenger door, so every time we go around a bend, she rocks against my side. Hm. Is there a curvier route to take down the mountains? One where she'll knock against me more?

"We can't stand too close," she goes on. "And, um. We need to fix our clothes first. Our hair, too. We look like..."

I bite back a laugh, grinning out at the trees lining the mountain road. The afternoon sun is golden, casting deep shadows between the trunks.

"Like we snuck out to roll around a hotel for a few hours?"

If only.

Priya blows out a breath. "Exactly. I don't want anyone to

113

think I'm sleeping with the boss."

That sobers me up. My smile fades, because I don't like thinking that either, not even as a rumor. I swear to god: Tom had better keep a polite distance, because Priya is *mine*. His assistant is off limits, now and forever.

"It'll be fine," I rasp. "I'll keep my hands off you in public, I promise."

"But only in public," Priya adds.

Hallelujah.

* * *

We get a few weird looks crossing the Landry & Co lobby, but that's all. Most folks go back to their own business, the women's heels clacking against the marble tiles, the men's voices carrying in a low rumble. Priya steps into the elevator first, wrinkling her nose at the creaky cage door, and she's so fucking cute that it kills me not to drag her against my chest, witnesses be damned.

I don't, obviously. I'm a man of my word, and I will never break a promise to Priya. What would be the point of me then?

"I hate this elevator," she mutters as we rise through the building in jerky motions. She smooths her burgundy dress for the millionth time, but no matter how much she fusses over our clothes, we're both covered in creases.

At least our mouths are less swollen. Priya braided her hair in the truck, and she refastened one of my shirt buttons, too. It was worth getting strangled by this collar to feel her knuckles brush my chest.

I nudge her shoulder. "It's my favorite part. The only old feature left in the building." She huffs, inching closer, and I

114

inhale deeply, trying to get a whiff of her hair. I learned in the mountains: Priya smells like oranges and cloves. "Could use some maintenance, though," I say after an extra loud clang. "Tom probably thinks all old elevators sound like a bag of saucepans dropped down the stairs."

Her lips press together. That's her fighting-a-laugh face, and it's my absolute favorite.

"You're a goddess," I say.

She snorts and elbows me, like I'm kidding around. I'm not.

The top floor is quiet, Tom's office door closed to hide the wreckage inside. It looks worse than it is back there—I'm almost done with the ad hoc renovations, and it's mostly paint smell and dust sheets and clutter. An hour to clean up, tops.

Meanwhile Priya's desk is so neat. There's a potted plant, like this office isn't a jungle already. I stop at the desk corner, flicking a pen.

She brushes past me, rolling her chair out, but I'm not ready to leave her yet. Not ready to be Fake Tom again, hidden away in another room, my longing for her vibrating through the walls.

"A moment please, Miss Dhawan."

Priya laughs and grips my shoulders as I take her waist, lifting her easily. When I set her down on the desk, the pen I flicked rolls onto the floor. Her legs widen, and soft thighs brush either side of my hips. Her dress rucks up, and I send a silent prayer of thanks to the heavens.

I'm a simple man. I know a blessing when I feel one.

And this time is nothing like those hours back in the mountains. Instead of jewel-toned sunshine and the whisper of trees, we're surrounded by electric light and the faint hum of Priya's computer.

Don't care. *She's* still unearthly, so beautiful with her smooth, tawny skin and brown eyes, her neat braid and wrinkled dress, and fuck. The way I feel about this woman is not normal.

After only a few days, I want to own her and be owned. Want to taste every inch of her skin, and catalog the sounds she makes in bed, and know what she's thinking at every minute of every day, for the rest of our lives.

Did I hit my head on the day we met?

If I did, I don't care.

And even in my own thoughts, I sound like a madman. If I don't keep a lid on this, I'll scare her away.

"Let's discuss your work performance."

Priya buries her laugh against my throat. "Nooo, this is a terrible idea for a role play."

"I am your *boss*, Miss Dhawan."

"You're going to make yourself jealous again, you big goof."

True. And... she noticed that?

Of course she did. Priya's quiet but observant. She reads people all the time—and I'm so open for her, it must be no work at all. If some people are hard to read, like a classic Russian novel, for Priya, I'm a picture book. I rhyme.

When she tilts her chin up, lips parting, my chest burns with triumph. Her mouth is still a tiny bit puffy from earlier. And kissing her again... it's like we brought the mountain sunshine back with us. Like we're still there together, tucked away from the world, where only the trees can hear us groan.

"Shh," Priya says as I kiss down her neck, even though *she's* the source of the whimpers. Whatever. I love this little hypocrite.

"Don't worry." My hands roam up and down her sides, squeezing her waist, cupping her breasts, finding her hips.

"We'll hear the elevator all the way from the ground floor."

I won't risk her. I'd never risk her.

We kiss again until my blood pounds in my veins; until there's nothing but animal urges in my brain. The desk creaks as her legs part wider. Soon enough, my fingertips brush the blue lace of her panties, and Priya tips back her head with a sigh.

She leans her palms on the desk, and watches me beneath heavy lidded eyes. Her hips twitch up, chasing my touch.

"Is this okay?" My heart thunders.

Priya's mouth quirks. "It's more than okay."

Thank fuck for that.

She's slick when I delve beneath the lace. Warm and wet and soft, her body calling me closer, and her breath catches each time I brush against her clit.

Perfection. Winding her braid around my free hand, I hold her in place with mock sternness, then press one finger inside her.

"Oh." Priya's eyes flutter, and the blush darkens on her cheeks. Her hips twitch up again, coaxing me deeper. "Oh, that feels…"

I inhale deeply, stroking her inner walls. She's softer than velvet here too. "Good?"

"*So* good. Oh, wow."

A man could get used to hearing things like that. I shift closer, adjust my wrist for a better angle, and Priya's computer screen flickers to life when her thigh knocks the mouse. One finger inside her. Two.

"Emmett," she gasps, and my name on her lips is pure music.

"Sweetheart." I graze her clit and stroke deeper at the same time, muffling her cries with a kiss. "Priya. My Priya."

We're lost in each other. Lost in this haze.

Maybe that's why we don't hear the footsteps in the office behind us, nor the creak of the door handle. Maybe that's where we go wrong.

"Em?" My brother's voice is a bucket of cold water down my spine. Priya goes rigid in my arms. My fingers are inside her.

Not now. Shit, not now.

"What are you—what the hell are you doing?" He gets louder. "Wait. Is that my assistant?"

Priya

❧⚬❧

Fired for screwing around with my boss's identical stand-in. That's a new one, surely. If I'm going down in disgrace, at least I'm original.

So humiliating. How did I get here? I'm the goody-two-shoes, not the girl who gets fired for hooking up at her desk. What was I thinking?

Well, I *wasn't* thinking. That much is obvious. And now I'm sprawled on our couch in my slobbiest sweatshirt and leggings, trying to numb the static in my head with a nature documentary about penguins.

It's not helping. One penguin got eaten by a shark, and I burst into tears. Even Rusty freaked out, wiping his sticky nose on my arm, trying to make me feel better.

"It's for the best," Maisie says for the dozenth time, her soft voice cutting through the sound of penguins squawking. She's already cooked dinner, talked everything over with me, and coaxed me through a yoga practice. Didn't really help, but god, I love her. "They took you for granted at that place. Now you can go on to better things."

"Ngh," I grunt. As if 'better things' will hire me with this in my reference. The only bosses who'll want me now are perverts.

It all happened so fast. Getting caught; getting fired. Emmett looked mad enough to tear down the Landry & Co building with his bare hands, but it's not his company. Not his call.

Emmett. God.

I wrap my arms around the cat on my chest, Rusty's pinprick claws needling my shoulder through my sweatshirt. He's fluffy and warm and his breath smells like chicken today. Cute but gross.

What is Emmett doing now? Does he hate me for causing trouble with his brother? Why hasn't he called? It's been *hours*. Bleurgh.

Best—then worst—day ever.

These penguins mate for life, the British narrator says, and I fling the nearest cushion at the TV. "Oh yeah? Good for them!"

Rusty meows and jumps down, trotting away to find a less dramatic cuddle. He heads down the hall for Fliss's bedroom, but since she's in there with her new man, he'll be crying at the door for a while.

"It's only been a few hours," Maisie says. "Emmett still might—"

She cuts off as our intercom buzzes, then raises an eyebrow at me. Her face is ghostly and delicate among the pile of blankets. Penguins waddle across the ice on screen.

"It's not him," I say as I get up. Need to keep my hopes low for my own sanity. "Bet you a dollar it's not."

Maisie shrugs, the blankets shifting. "I'll take that bet."

I saw Emmett earlier today—got up close and personal with

120

him, learned how he smells and feels, and how he sounds when he presses a finger inside me. But as I tug our apartment door open, for a split second, the handsome man in a black Henley and jeans seems like a stranger.

Then his mouth twists. "Priya," he says, so soft and mournful, and it's *him*, it's my Emmett in his own freaking clothes, and he came after all. He came for me.

I walk into his arms, giddy with relief.

He squeezes me tight, chin resting on my head.

"I talked to Tom. Well, yelled at him, really. You can have your job back if you want it." Emmett sighs as I shake my head, but he doesn't argue. How could I ever work there again after what his brother saw? After he already fired me once? "Then he'll give you a glowing reference, as you deserve."

I'm not sure about the deserving part, not after today, but I'll take it. Lord, I will take it. Calm washes over me, and I melt against Emmett's chest.

"Thank you." My words are muffled by his shirt. It's faded black cotton, soft and worn and comfortable, and it's so luxurious somehow to see him *out* of those suits. "Thank you so much."

But Emmett groans, rocking me from side to side. "Don't thank me, sweetheart, whatever you do. I caused all this mess."

That's so unfair! "No, you didn't. We caused it together."

Emmett kisses the top of my head. "Can I take you somewhere?"

He can take me to a haunted gas station if he wants to. He can take me to the world's creepiest motel—I don't care where we're going, as long as Emmett's there.

I nod, cheek squished against his chest. "Do I need to change?"

"No. You're perfect, Priya."

Only this man would think so, but then... maybe this man is all I need.

* * *

The ex-chapel in the mountains looks different at night. The stained glass windows look black; the pale stone glows in the moonlight. When we hop down from the truck, slamming the doors, at least the pine-scented air is familiar.

An owl hoots. "Wait here," Emmett says softly, the breeze whispering through the trees. "Call out if you need me, okay? I'll be two minutes."

"Okay."

Listen: I will *not* be a giant baby. I will not cling to his hand and wail for him not to leave me out here. I am a grown woman, damn it, and I can handle two minutes out at night on my own.

My back rests against the warm truck as Emmett disappears inside. Tipping my head back, I gaze up at the stars overhead: a sky dusted with diamonds. You can see so many more up here than down in the city.

Down in the city, where I got fired today.

"Alright." Emmett's voice makes me jump, but his hand slides around mine. He tugs me to the deck, leading me carefully up the steps.

It's just like this morning, except we grip each other's hands like a lifeline, all shyness gone, and the safe path through the rooms is lit by candles in little glass jars. Their warm glow spreads up the walls, tiny flames dancing. It smells faintly of smoke now as well as sawdust.

"Why here?" I murmur, though I'm not mad about it—

especially when Emmett leads me into the room where he's piled pillows and blankets and made a big circle of hundreds of candles. When did he get those? Did he come here earlier?

"Because you said it's your dream house." Emmett leads me to the blanket nest, then hovers at the edges, suddenly awkward. "So, as of this morning, I'm fixing it up for you. Unless you change your mind and want something else, anyway." He scratches his chin, stubble rasping. "That's fine too."

"Oh my god." Tears blur my eyes as I tug him down to the blankets. Emmett comes easily, boots thunking against the floorboards. He sits with his knees bent, too big for his own set-up, and he's so beautiful with his pale blue eyes and dark hair and comfy old clothes.

I straddle his lap. All around us, candles flicker.

There's that wicked smile.

"So you'll still have me, Priya?" His palms slide under my clothes, coasting over bare skin, and he chuckles at my full-body shiver. Um, yes I'll have him. Today and every day for the rest of my life, if I can help it. "Even after I got you fired?"

I draw his bottom lip between my teeth, tugging until he hisses, then soothe it with a kiss. "Even then."

And our breaths start soft, but they get quick and ragged. Our kisses start sweet, but soon enough, we're all teeth and tongue. Emmett grips my hips, surging up beneath me with a grunt, and he's touching me everywhere, tasting my throat, my chest, yanking my sweatshirt over my head and tossing it out of range of the candles.

"Beautiful." My bra goes next, which is just as well, because dingy white cotton doesn't look good even in candlelight. Oops. "Ah, fuck, Priya. Your tits could make a grown man weep."

Is that a good thing? Judging by the reverent way Emmett cups and kneads me, and by his hungry groan when he sucks my nipple into his mouth… yes. It's a very good thing.

The room spins, and I grip the back of his head, thighs suddenly wobbling beneath me. I'm *aching*, and with every pull of his mouth, the tingling between my legs gets even worse. His mouth is so hot and wet.

Emmett moves to the other nipple, and I bite back a wail of frustration. Feels so *good*, so impossibly good, and it's nowhere near enough.

"Touch me." I grab his wrist and shove his hand between my thighs. There's zero grace in me right now, only the bone deep need to feel this man everywhere. "Emmett, touch me."

He hums against my breast, licking and sucking, but his fingers slide beneath the waistband of my leggings.

Fingertips brush. My hips buck forward. He's teasing me there, grazing me where I need him, but it's not enough. Not enough, damn it! Gripping his hair, I yank his head away.

Emmett sits back, breathing hard. His blue eyes are nearly black, swallowed up by his hungry pupils, and his lips are reddened and shiny. His stubble has burned a path over my skin.

"I was enjoying that," he says, so calm. And that mock sternness, that dominant edge, makes burning need twist through me like a stomach cramp.

"Emmett." My fist lands on his chest, pressing in warning. How is he still clothed? "I swear to god. If you don't fuck me soon, I'll scream."

His grin is blinding, his skin golden in the candlelight glow. Rough hands guide me up, yanking my leggings and underwear down my legs, then he tugs them off my feet.

"What about your clothes?" I ask as Emmett unbuckles his belt and works his jeans open, because he draws out his cock—thick and long and weeping a bead of moisture—then settles back on his palms, job done.

"No," he says idly, rolling his head back and watching me with a lazy grin. "I think I'll fuck you like this the first time. You've seen me in those monkey suits so many times, Priya—let's really drive home which twin you're with."

Ha. Is he honestly still jealous? Still worried about the twin thing?

"Oh, please." When I kneel on either side of Emmett's hips, the blankets cushion the floorboards. He's so warm and sturdy beneath me—a masterpiece of muscle and bone. "You could wear anything your brother owns, and I'd still know it was you. And vice versa."

He blows out a breath. "You say the sweetest things."

A hand in my hair tugs my head to the side. There's the scrape of teeth on my neck, and a hot stripe of tongue, and I'm so distracted I nearly leap a foot into the air when fingertips find my clit.

"You're mine." Each rough circle of his fingers drives me wild, bucking against his hold; each thrashing movement burns my scalp where he grips my hair. But it's perfect, so perfect, and when he presses a thick finger inside me, I wail in relief. "That's it, sweetheart. Tell me you're mine."

"I'm yours, Emmett." His snarl of approval must addle my brain, because I add: "Did you know penguins mate for life?"

Emmett pauses, one finger wedged deep in my body. Outside, the breeze taps against the windows, but at least up here in the mountains, there's only one witness if I die of embarrassment.

"Oh?" he says at last, thumb swirling over my clit. I buck and grit my teeth, cheeks flaming. "That's nice. I do too."

He does?

It's too late. I'll be dead of humiliation. My whole life, I've been waiting for the right man to have sex with, and now that I've found him… oh god. I can't believe I said that. So lame.

"Priya," Emmett says, voice thick with humor. "Stop fretting. That was sweet. *You're* sweet. Now let's wrap up this meltdown because I really, really need to fuck you."

Okay, yeah.

I need that too.

"Tell no one," I warn, rocking my hips to get him moving again.

Emmett kisses my throat, finger crooking inside me. "Who would I tell?"

"I don't know. Your brother?"

The animal noise that tears out of him—the way his body tenses, hands rougher, voice hard—I know it's messed up, but it takes my breath away. I cling to his shoulders, so thrilled as he says, "*Never*. He'll never get a single goddamn detail about you. If he ever even *looks* at you the wrong way—"

"So jealous," I tease, laughing happily as Emmett draws his finger out and shoves my thighs wider. He guides me to his shaft, jaw rock hard and suddenly so serious.

I don't mind. I *love* that he wants me this badly, that he's snapping and snarling, so possessive over me.

That I'm treasured. His.

Despite his tensed muscles and the violence thrumming under his skin, Emmett is gentle as he nudges inside me. "Go slowly," he clips out as I sink down one inch, then two. "Priya, go slowly."

126

Priya

Tipping my head back, relishing the sting, I ignore him and sink all the way down onto my man.

Emmett

"Priya!" Her name tears out of me; my hips surge up. She's taken me by surprise and now I'm fighting with my own body, wrestling down the urge to fill her up. My balls are drawn up tight, and I'm harder than stone. "Jesus Christ."

She laughs, arms winding around my neck, and grinds against my lap.

My shaft throbs inside her.

"This nearly lasted two seconds." When I grab a fistful of her hair, Priya smirks. She *wants* to push me; wants to ride out the consequences. Literally. "You'll pay for that, imp. Not such a good girl now, are you?"

Her teeth are on my throat. Her laugh is warm against my neck. She's so wild and free like this, so blissfully unself-conscious, working herself over my shaft and crying out in pleasure.

Priya Dhawan is a force of nature. Of course she is.

Can't believe I get to touch her. To taste her. To do *this*.

For the rest of our lives, I'll prove how much I adore her. But first...

I spank her nipples lightly, more to shock her than to hurt, and as Priya cries out and rides me harder, they flush a deeper brown. A blush stains her chest and throat, and her thighs are damp with sweat, and wherever I touch her, the muscles shiver.

I grip her ass and squeeze. Part her cheeks and fuck her deeper. Move her roughly, guiding her over my lap, belt buckle scraping against the floor—just because I can and I know she likes it, and every stroke into her channel sends red-hot sparks crackling down my spine.

Priya likes me in charge, bossing her around. Nothing fake about it, not right now.

"Mine," I grunt. "Mine."

Blankets snag against the floorboards, and my boot heel knocks a candle. It rolls to one side, little flame guttering out, a wisp of smoke dancing away.

"*Mine.*"

It's the only word left in my brain, and I grit it through clenched teeth. My abs ache, and I'm sweating into my clothes, and every roll of Priya's hips makes me want to pound on the floorboards and howl.

"If I'm yours, prove it," Priya says, so breathless, already grinning. She whoops as I roll us over, laying her back on the blankets then shoving her thighs wide apart.

I hold her there, splayed open. Loom over her like a ravenous beast, the open edges of my jeans dragging against her skin.

"The fuck did you just say?"

She laughs as I thrust deep inside. It chokes off into a moan as I ride her without mercy, muscles flexing, jaw clenched, fighting against my own rueful smile.

She's so mischievous, under all that good girl poise. So playful. God, I love this woman.

Priya arches against the blankets when I rub her clit. She lets out a string of curses, eyes squeezed shut and head rocking side to side.

And I don't hold back. I keep riding, keep rubbing. Change angle to hit a spot inside that steals her breath, and then pinch her clit, because why go easy on her? That's not what she wants from me, not what she needs.

Priya's mouth drops open in a silent scream.

Yeah. That's more like it.

The beautiful imp asked for this, and now I'll wring her out. I'll feel her come on my cock, and I'll commit every damn detail to memory. And when Priya walks away from here tonight— bowlegged, if I have my way—she'll know down to her bones that I'm her man. Me. No goddamn *if* about it.

"Oh my *god*." Her nails score my back, blunted only by my shirt, and her legs wrap tight around my waist, squeezing. It puts my wrist at a weird angle, but I keep rubbing.

No mercy.

And… it's like a bomb going off. You know in action movies when there's a huge explosion, and the camera zooms out miles and miles to show a shock wave rippling over long grass? That's what it's like when Priya comes.

Her body locks up, suddenly rigid. She breathes in little pants through her nose. And though her center is completely still, these shock waves coast through the rest of her body, trembling her muscles and making her squeak.

Perfection. I ride her through it all, muscles aching, dragging it out as long as I can, and once she slumps into the blanket nest,

I shove deep inside her and let my head rest on her shoulder. I'm breathing hard.

With her palms tracing wobbly circles on my back, my shaft twitches and fills Priya up in long spurts, over and over.

It's the most peaceful I've felt in my whole damn life.

"That tickles," she says against my ear. I turn and kiss her, gentle and deep, and we're sticky and sweaty but I don't care.

I'm telling you: paradise.

This is only the beginning.

* * *

One year later

"Just promise me if you don't like it, you'll say so. There are so many other houses, Priya. So many places we could live. I swear to god, I won't mind if you don't like this one."

My wife's hand on my thigh usually calms me right away, but today is different. I clench the steering wheel, guiding my truck up the mountain path, and send up silent thanks for the pine-fresh breeze washing through the windows to cool my cheeks.

What if she hates it? Or no, I could deal with that, but what if Priya hates it and is too polite to say so? What if I trap the love of my life in a home she hates, out here in the mountains?

"I promise I'll say something." For once, my girl is serious, sensing how much her answer means to me. "But Emmett? I'm going to love it."

We'll see.

It's a bright morning as we drive up to the old chapel. The path is smooth, with no more potholes or trenches, and Priya smiles at the stained glass windows, sparkling clean and jewel-toned in the sun.

"Oh my god, look at that deck! I remember this whole place was such a ruin."

Not anymore. If I'm fixing up a house for my wife, you'd better believe she's getting the best of everything. Best materials, best workmanship, best intentions. The best of the best.

Tiny twigs crunch beneath my boots as I round the truck. I open Priya's door, helping her down.

"We can go visit the nearest town after this, to make sure you still like it. It's a mile away, but it's a good size for the mountains. And they have a school and a doctor's office a grocery store and all that life crap."

"Life crap," Priya repeats, fighting a smile. "Good to know."

The deck stairs are solid, with a hand-built table and chairs by the rail, the wood stained to weather the outdoors.

That set gave me the devil's own splinters, but it's all worth it when Priya coos over it, one hand cradling her bump through her yellow sundress. "Oh, we could drink coffee out here in the morning! And eat outside in the summer. Maybe there's room for a barbecue...?"

She turns to me, eyes shining with hope.

"Way ahead of you." Thank god. "It's around the back. And I've started baby-proofing the inside, come and see what you think..."

Already, I'm breathing easier, shoulders relaxed. Priya really does love it, I can tell, so this tour feels less like a horrible test, and more like a privilege. I'm showing my wife the home I built for her and our child.

And if she likes it enough to show her approval in certain

physical ways… so be it. I will bear that burden.

Birds chatter in the branches, and the breeze rustles the trees. The sunshine tints pink and purple as we step inside, and it's warmer in here, and so peaceful.

"I built some wood stuff by hand, but I figured you'd want to choose most of the furniture yourself. Curtains and sofas and whatnot."

Priya's hand finds mine. "Good instinct."

Leading her through our new home, I really don't mind. Priya picked me, didn't she? So she clearly has excellent taste.

"Can we put up bird feeders?" she asks, watching a wood-pecker flit past the window. She already knows the answer to that.

"Priya?" I squeeze her fingers, my chest so warm. "This is our kingdom now. We can do whatever the hell we want."

III

Whole Lotta Grump

Description

H e's surly and mean. He makes grown men cower. And I give him massages every week.

Everyone in this city has heard of Hudson Katz—the Midas man. Every project he touches turns to gold.

But he's not famous for his success. Or not only for that, anyway. No, Mr Katz is famous for being a giant, grade A *grump*.

That's where I come in. My healing hands; my soothing demeanor. It's my job to help the big grouch relax.

Except he's different with me. So real and raw.

And touching him feels so good… I don't ever want to stop.

Maisie

t first glance, the Midas Inc skyscraper looks like any other building in this city. All glass and shiny steel; sharp edges and straight lines. Bustling with people in suits, who yell into their phones and guzzle coffee like it's the elixir of life.

When you step into the lobby, it's barely any quieter than the street. Sure, outside cabbies lean on their horns and garbage trucks rumble along, but in here, people go about their days with LOUD URGENCY. Verging on panic.

No wonder they called me in.

If the minions are this stressed, I'm surprised Hudson Katz hasn't keeled over yet. Surprised he hasn't burst a vein.

After I'm done with the boss, they should set me on the underlings next. Every single person in this dust-free, deafening skyscraper could use a back rub. I guarantee it.

They bark at each other, power walking past as I drift across the lobby. I prod the elevator button and wait, humming under my breath.

It's always strange coming here. Strange walking into any of my clients' offices, frankly. Like visiting another planet. So many of these big, powerful CEOs are stressing themselves into an early grave, and though I'll certainly try to help, I couldn't relate to anyone less.

What's the point of all this, you know? What's it all for? A few extra zeroes on a screen?

Please. They should try the waffle truck in the downtown city park. Now *that's* something worth selling your soul.

The elevator rises, floor after floor, so quick that I get that swoopy, roller coaster feeling in my stomach. Or maybe it's because I'm two minutes away from Hudson Katz. Could be that too.

Fluffing my hair in the elevator mirror, I smile politely at the workers who bustle in and out on different floors—then pinch my cheeks, aiming for some color, though I'm still pale beneath my freckles.

Will Hudson be glad to see me? Does he like these appointments?

It's always so hard to tell.

But as I tug my sky blue tunic straight, excitement fizzes under my skin—because *I* look forward to this appointment all week, counting down the days until I'm alone with Hudson Katz again.

Talking to him.

Touching him.

In a professional way, obviously. I clear my throat, glancing around guiltily, but no one can hear my thoughts. Duh. And even if they could, I doubt these busy bees would care. Bet plenty of them have the hots for the boss. When he looks like that, who wouldn't?

They step off the elevator one by one, click-clacking away in their heels or striding off in buffed leather shoes, until I'm left all alone with my reflection. The Maisie in the mirror looks excited—but she purses her lips and waggles a finger.

"Don't be weird." My voice bounces around the metal box. "Don't drool all over him. That's not part of the service."

Right.

Every week, I give myself this pep talk. Then every week, I step into Hudson Katz's penthouse office... and lose my freaking mind.

No. *No.*

This time, I'll be better. I won't think a single unprofessional thought about the handsome grump. I'll rub his shoulders, soothe his muscles, and get gone.

* * *

Hudson Katz is always fully dressed when I arrive. Obviously, in any other job that would be standard, but I'm a massage therapist. When I meet with a client, they're often already in a robe.

The appointments are expensive, you know? And they want their money's worth.

Not Hudson. He stands by the huge glass window in his office in a charcoal suit, arms folded over his chest, staring out at the city skyline. It's a sunny spring day, with a cool wind and puffs of white cloud. Beautiful.

Hudson glares like the sunshine offends him.

"Hey," I call, locking the door behind me. Once I trust a client, I always prefer a locked door. It helps them unwind; stops them from worrying about some underling bursting in

140

and seeing their boss in nothing but a towel. "You ready to relax, Mr Katz?"

Hudson grunts, still staring out at the spring day. He makes no move to undress, but the massage table is set up ready in the center of the floor, complete with a folded white towel. In the wall-length tank opposite the boss's desk, little fish flit up to the glass, investigating the new furniture.

Did Hudson set up the table and fetch the towel? Or does he get an assistant to do it?

Either way, the sight of that table brings a lump to my throat. See, *this* is why I get all tingly coming to see this grouch: because of all my fancy clients, of all the rich and powerful in this city, only Hudson Katz insists on keeping a massage table in his office so I won't have to lug one all the way here on the subway.

Our first appointment, he was so mad when he saw me huffing and puffing through the doorway. "How far did you bring that?" he demanded.

His very first bark at me. Historic.

Anyway, I told him how far, and he banned me from ever carrying my table all that way again. Sent me home with his driver, too. Swoon.

"Your minions seem extra stressy today."

This is how our time together goes: I chat, Hudson scowls into the distance. Pausing by his huge desk, I drop my tote bag on the glass and snap a hair tie onto my wrist, then join him at the window. The top of my head doesn't reach his shoulder.

We're already so high up here. Like gods.

And he's a foot higher. The godliest.

Muscles bulge against suit sleeves where his arms are crossed; Hudson's jaw is harder than granite. With his dark hair and dark eyes and that thundercloud demeanor, it's no wonder everyone in this building is scared of this man. It feels like he could yell and the earth would crack apart.

"You ready to strip, Mr Katz?"

He always needs coaxing. Needs to be teased out of his angry shell.

I don't mind. I like it.

Hudson blows out a harsh breath, then frowns down at me. I smile back, tying my hair into a ponytail.

"My left shoulder is stiff," he says, that low voice of his making me shiver.

"Okay." Silence rings through the office, and Hudson doesn't move—just towers over me, all broody and beautiful. "Can I take a look?"

The big boss jolts, like the suggestion is such a shock. Like he doesn't pay to get me here each week. It's funny: he may be the Midas man, may be rich and powerful as all get out, but every single massage appointment seems to take him by surprise.

Like he can't quite believe that he let me in again. Can't fathom that we're here once more. Wasting his precious minutes on human contact, when all those lines of zeroes are waiting on his computer screen.

"Now?" Hudson asks, tone grim. Always so reluctant to get started.

I will not find that sweet. I will not find that sweet.

"Now," I agree with a nod. "So we have enough time for the massage."

Another grunt. The boss steps away from the giant window, and I squint down at a vendor cart on the street far below, trying to distract myself from the whisper of clothes behind me. Giving him privacy, though god knows this man's enormous

142

chest is seared into my brain in high definition. I could sketch it by memory—could summon the image of his nipples in a heartbeat.

Soooo. What is that old guy selling on the corner down there? Hot dogs? Bet it's hot dogs.

Cotton slithers over skin; shoes thump against the rug. I stare down at the vendor, eyes dry, forgetting to blink.

With only my ears focused on the man behind me, I hear each of his steady breaths, each step across the floor. The creak of the massage table, and the faint rustle as he unfolds the towel and drapes it over his lap.

Hudson Katz needs an extra large towel. Just sayin'.

"Ready," he mutters.

Unknotting my fingers, I take a deep breath—then turn around with a bright smile.

The sight of his bare body always punches me in the ovaries. That vast, sculpted expanse of golden brown skin, dusted with dark hair; those ridged abs and the cut of his hips. So manly and strong and *gah*.

I want to poke him. Want to rub my whole face against his belly and blow a wet raspberry on the skin; want to pet his armpit hair and tweak his nose and pinch his cheeks like that old Russian lady on the subway. Want to roll in his pheromones like a puppy in leaves.

God. I want to *annihilate* this grump. Just… fuss over him until he explodes.

And some instinct tells me that despite his riches, Hudson Katz has never been doted on before. Not truly. He wouldn't know what hit him.

"So, your left shoulder," I say instead as I cross to my tote bag. *Act normal, you weirdo.* The bottle of oil is heavy as I snap the lid open. Oil pools in my palm, and I set it down with a thump on the desk. "Any other points of tension?"

"My neck," he says, low voice drifting across the room to meet me. He's flat on his back, glaring up at the ceiling. After the hustle and bustle downstairs, this office is an oasis: fish dart between plants in the tank by the wall, their colorful scales flashing, and the hum of the filter is soothing. "And my left hamstring. And my right side, between the ribs."

Poor, tense King Midas. "You should work less," I tell him, warming the oil between my palms. It's scented with citrus blossom. "And try yoga."

The look he shoots me could incinerate a man at twenty paces. Seriously, I've seen his underlings *run* from that look, eyes panicked, cheeks flushed, ready to sprint to the nearest job opening—or to sob in the bathroom.

Doesn't work on me. Since day one, I've been immune, and I fight a smile, approaching the table. "Or not."

When I reach out my hands, we both hold our breath. The air shivers through the room, and even the fish go still, fins fluttering with anticipation.

Has it only been a week? It feels more like years since I put my hands on this man. Like a geological era has passed. Does Hudson miss me between appointments, the way I miss him? Is this the highlight of his week too? Or am I a total lost cause?

When I touch his arm, fingers sliding along his bicep, my insides quiver.

Hudson Katz lets out a soft hiss, and time speeds up again.

"Okay, Mr Katz." My voice wobbles. He scowls past me at the ceiling, no sign that he's affected by my touch at all, damn it. Did I imagine that hiss? "Let's begin."

Hudson

❦

L et me be clear: a massage is my idea of hell. Stripping down for a stranger? Interrupting my work day? Having someone else's hands all over my body, slicking me up with oil that never fully washes off on the first try? Worst of all: making polite fucking conversation?

Kill me now.

I only caved and allowed Maisie in that first time because my back was ninety percent gristle: stiff and knotted and aching like hell, so bad I couldn't focus. The Midas Inc board booked her, and I let them. Call it a moment of weakness.

That's how she wound up in my office the first time, smiling and chattering away as she set up the table, all wavy black hair and dove gray eyes. So sweet and pretty and calm. The kind of girl you might see on a postcard from Switzerland, wearing lederhosen and swinging a pail of fresh milk, beaming in the mountain air. So gut-wrenchingly wholesome.

Meeting Maisie for the first time was like being slapped in the face with a rainbow. All the other times... our weekly appointment over the last three months…

I can't explain it. I *won't* explain it. But I need to see her on a regular basis, and that's non-negotiable.

For the record, I still hate massages. But Maisie's hands on me aren't so bad. She's excellent at her job—the best in the city, naturally—but more than that, I can't shake the feeling that it's *me* she's touching. Not just any other body stretched out beneath a towel. Me.

With any other massage therapist, I'd hate that even more. But with Maisie, it's exactly what I crave.

"Sir?" My assistant Carlton frowns and peers closer, a pen tapping against his notepad. He's been briefing me for the day, standing in front of my desk in his purple suit, but when he says my name, I can't remember the last five minutes. Everything is a haze.

Have I been staring into the fish tank all that time, thinking about my massage therapist? Or has he just been that boring?

"What?" I snap.

Carlton straightens, fingers tightening on his pen. "I said that the big meeting is this afternoon. The one with the Spanish division? You told me to set it up months ago, sir. Anyway, they flew in yesterday and you're set to meet at 3pm—"

Maisie o'clock. Unacceptable.

"Reschedule it," I say, and if I were a kinder person, I'd care that Carlton looks like he might faint. "Push it forward or back by two hours. I don't care which."

"But sir—"

"It wasn't a suggestion."

Carlton huffs out a breath, then nods miserably. Thinking of Maisie, I attempt a smile. That's what she'd do, right? She'd smile and make everyone feel better, but when I try it, my face feels wrong. Unnatural.

"Oh," my assistant says, stumbling back like he's seen a ghost. The notebook trembles in his hands. Too toothy, maybe? "Oh, well, I'd better go deal with that."

"Thank you, Carlton."

Another baffled glance, then his purple suit hurries through my doorway. I wait for the soft click of the door, the blissful wave of silence, then let my forced smile drop away.

Fish dance back and forth in the tank opposite me. Plants undulate in tiny currents. The glow from the tank spills into the room, warring with the morning sunshine, and I know that Carlton finds that glow eerie, but I love it.

Sometimes—and I'd never admit this out loud—I wish I was in there too. As a crab, maybe, or one of those glass-cleaning water snails.

Peaceful. Unstressed. No deadlines or people or pressure.

…But no Maisie either.

I straighten in my desk chair, clearing my throat. It's a stupid fantasy.

* * *

"The Spanish division, huh?" Maisie drops her tote bag on my desk. Her belongings clatter against the glass, barely muffled by the fabric, and something knocks my keyboard askew. "Well, nobody expects the Spanish Inquisition."

I frown from my place by the window. I'm missing something. "Excuse me?"

Maisie's mouth twitches. "Nothing. Don't worry."

Ugh. I shouldn't have mentioned that meeting at all. Now she knows that I rescheduled for her; that our appointments are my number one priority, even above work concerns. What will she do with that knowledge? How could she use it against me?

"Look how sour you are today!" Maisie grins as she crosses the office to join me, her hips swaying as she walks. That sky blue tunic she wears nips in at her waist, hinting at her small curves, and she wears glittery pink sneakers with leggings.

With every step, her sneakers catch the light. Like fish scales.

And when she pulls her dark waves up into a ponytail, the hair tie held briefly between her teeth, my heart shudders—then slams against my ribs, pounding faster.

That *neck*. It's so elegant. Her skin looks soft and creamy, and those freckles disappear beneath her tunic. How far do they go? Is her whole body freckled under those clothes?

"I'm not sour," I say at last, groping for my half of the conversation. What is wrong with me? I focus for hours on end at work, but the second this woman walks in the room, my thoughts scatter. "I'm impatient. Let's get this over with, please—I'm a busy man."

Maisie's smile flickers.

She looks... hurt.

Fuck.

"Well, we're waiting on you, Midas man." My massage therapist's words are teasing, but she won't look at me. She turns to the window, folding her arms, and that's my signal to undress and get on the table. Guess we're done chatting.

"Maisie," I say. My chest is tight.

A glittery pink sneaker taps against the floor. Her shoulders are tense, and I hate that. Hate that I've brought her down to my miserable level. She's still waiting for me to go away and strip, to fall back into our roles as massage therapist and client, where I can be as brash as I like and she won't care at all because I'm nothing to her. A paycheck, that's all.

Why am I like this? Why can't I be kind to the one person I care about? The one person I want to keep around.

"Maisie," I say again. "I'm sorry." The word is foreign on my tongue, but for her, I'll say anything. Anything at all. "I didn't mean that. You're right, I am sour today."

And I'm a prick, that's what I am. A lonely, grumpy, unbearable jerk who's only good for making money. How did I get here? Where did I go wrong in life? What kind of monster could make this woman sad?

I blow out a harsh breath, tugging at my shirt collar. If I've pushed Maisie away, there's no hope for me. Everyone else, I could boss around or pay them off; I could buy or bully their good opinion back. Not her. "Can we start over?"

Her lips purse. She casts me a glance—then does a double take, gray eyes going wide with concern.

Do I look that wrecked? After the world's tiniest argument? It's kind of funny: I regularly get in screaming matches as part of my work, but the smallest tiff with Maisie makes me want to tear my own skin off. I'm falling to pieces here, and she sees it.

"Okay," she says softly, her touch ghosting over my arm. "Okay, let's start over. The Spanish division, huh? Well, nobody expects the Spanish Inquisition."

"Ha." I force a smile—but unlike Carlton, Maisie doesn't flinch. "Very funny. I completely understand that joke."

And... her laugh is pure sunshine. It spills over me, warming my skin; it soothes my tight chest. My smile relaxes and turns real. Is that all it takes? Is everything fixed?

Yes, I can tell from the sparkle in her eyes: we're okay, and I can breathe easy again. Thank god.

"Strip, mister." This time, her order is fond, and as I turn away, already flicking my shirt buttons open, Maisie watches me go. Is it my imagination, or do her eyes linger before she turns back to the window?

Surely not. Maisie's a goddess, and I'm a snarling beast locked in his tower. I've proved that again today.

She wasn't staring. It's wishful thinking, nothing more.

Maisie

"**I** can't believe you massage Hudson Katz."

My roommate Fliss raises her ancient cat overhead, cooing and making kissy faces. It's a Friday night, and our living room is a sea of take out containers, adult coloring books, and pencil sets. The end credits of a trashy movie are paused on the TV screen, and I'm a little woozy from the half-drunk pitcher of mojitos.

Since both my roomies fell head over heels in love with their men, they've gotten busier. We've had to schedule in girls' nights to get our fix. And I'm pint-sized, so a single drink makes me float up to the clouds.

I wasn't ready for this ambush, though.

"God, I know, right?" Sitting beside her on the sofa, Priya reaches up to scratch Rusty behind the ear. He purrs and purrs, flecks of brown fur raining onto their laps. "*The* Hudson Katz. I'd be so scared."

The armchair rustles as I shift, a pink-tipped pencil dropping to the floor. "He's not scary. When you get to know him,

Hudson's not like that at all."

Not with me, anyway. Burrowing into the armchair cushions, I pretend I don't feel my cheeks flaming.

They both give me knowing looks.

I wet my lips and taste lime.

Car horns blare down in the street, and our 'cocktails and chill' playlist hums from the speaker on the bookcase. Our apartment is warm and cozy, lit by the soft glow of table lamps.

"King Midas," Priya sing-songs, flicking her braid over one shoulder. She's in one of her boyfriend's huge plaid shirts, the flannel flecked with white paint. "Poor King Midas; everything he touches turns to gold. Are you gold yet, Maisie?"

Fliss snickers. "I bet bits of her are. Look at that blush!"

"He's never touched me," I say quickly. "Not once. Why would he? *I'm* the massage therapist in the room."

But… now that they mention it, *why* hasn't he touched me? Wracking my brain, I can't think of a single time Hudson Katz has reached out to me. Not for a friendly pat on the shoulder. Not even a businesslike handshake. It's been months. Isn't that weird?

Doesn't he want to? Is he secretly repulsed? I mean, I spend all week between our appointments so desperate for the feel of his skin. So eager to feel his pulse and his strong bones and those silky dark chest hairs. Jonesing for my fix.

Even now, my fingers tingle with how badly I want to touch him again. I squeeze them into fists, knuckles aching.

"He's got these fish," I say out of nowhere, distracting myself by talking crap. "In a giant tank in his office. They're really pretty."

"Nice," Fliss says, cuddling Rusty against her chest, either not noticing or not caring when he starts licking her pink-streaked hair. "We like fishies, don't we, handsome?" Then the girls are off, talking about the movie we watched, and I'm left plucking at a loose thread on the armchair. Agitated.

I'm not done talking about Hudson yet—but I've got no reason to bring him up again. He's not my boyfriend, or even a reasonable crush. He's a client.

Professionalism. Bleurgh.

Leaning forward, I pour myself another mojito. Half-melted ice and a chunk of lime bob in my glass, and I stab them with my paper straw. The end's gone all soggy. Are there no happy endings?

"Why are you scowling like that, Maisie?" Fliss grins. "Guess crankiness is catching. Hudson Katz has rubbed off on you."

"If only," I say, the mojitos making me bold, then clap my hand over my mouth. But they both whoop, cackling together on the sofa—and, okay. My mouth twitches behind my palm. Okay. I'm very lucky, my life is great, and this bad mood has gone on long enough. My doomed crush on Hudson Katz can settle down.

Because what's a little heartbreak? I have everything I need right here. Closing my eyes, I draw in a deep breath, and cast my mind back to the meditation class I took last year, where they were super into visualization. Can't hurt to try, right?

I count to three, then imagine myself unbuckling a heavy velvet cloak. Feel the weight drop away from my shoulders, taking all my angst with it.

When my eyes flutter open, I'm a million times lighter. Nailed it. Placing my drink down, I reach for Rusty. "Gimme."

The scruffy brown fur ball is passed along a train of cooing women. He's the real Lothario around here, and I settle back in the armchair, his purr vibrating against my chest. Tiny claws needle through my shirt, and hey, that's second base with Rusty. Is that a win?

"You," Priya says, fixing me with a stern look, "should tell Hudson Katz you like him."

I snort. "Hardly. He's my favorite client. And Hudson doesn't do *feelings*, everyone in the city knows that. Too sticky," I add, but they don't run with the joke. They're both suddenly serious, watching me.

The speaker hums. Air bubbles cling to the sides of my glass, and the cat rustles in my arms, purring louder.

"Maybe he would for you." Fliss's voice is soft, and I bury my face in Rusty's fur, where it's warm and safe and musty. Our sweet, musty Rusty.

Yes, maybe Hudson would. Or maybe I'd lose the tiny bit of the Midas man I already have.

He's so closed off to the world. So impenetrable. And with the awkward smiles he gives me, with the apology he made this afternoon, I already have more of Hudson Katz than I had any right to hope for. More than anyone else gets, that's for sure.

Gratitude, that's the trick. I can't let myself get greedy.

* * *

"You're very calming, did you know that?" Despite his words, Hudson's thick eyebrows are pinched. Eyes closed, he frowns at the ceiling as I massage his forearm.

So much bare skin. So many muscles. God, he's so *huge*, laid out on the massage table like a surly giant on a slab.

When Hudson shifts, the folded white towel draped over his lap brushes my hip. I swallow.

"And yet you're so tense." Seriously, his forearm is rock-hard, corded with muscle and tendons. It's heavy when I slide my fingers underneath, slicking oil over the skin. "Are you sure these massages even help?"

As soon as I ask the question, I want to snatch it back—want to stuff it back in my mouth and chew it to pieces. What the hell am I doing? What if Hudson agrees, and I never see him again?

There's a long pause, where the only sounds are our steady breaths and the hum of the fish tank. Normally, I play spa-themed music from a portable speaker for these appointments, but with Hudson I never do. I like hearing the soft sound of our skin brushing together, because I am a tragic weirdo.

"I'm sure," he rasps at last.

Whew. My shoulders drop down from my ears.

Here's another thing I do differently with Hudson Katz compared to my other clients: for most of the appointment, I have him lay on his back. Oh, he'll turn over eventually so I can dig all the knots from his shoulder blades, but for the first half of our time together, I like being able to see his face.

Eyes closed, jaw ticking. Exposed in some ways, closed off in others.

So dreamy.

Everyone else, I start them face down—and mostly keep them there, unless they have tension in their front. Because they don't have Hudson Katz's face, do they? Their closed-eyed scowls don't make my heart pound.

Meanwhile, with Hudson, I'm plenty flustered. Every time I see this man, clothed or unclothed, my mouth goes dry.

And touching him? Smoothing my way along his chest like this, digging into the hard planes of muscle? Feeling his heartbeat thud against my palm? Forget it.

My thumb brushes his nipple.

Hudson grunts, frowning harder.

"Sorry," I whisper. Bad Maisie.

I spend the rest of the massage with my lips pressed together, extra careful of where I touch. Like coloring in the lines.

Hudson

The whole time I've known Maisie, she's been a walking ray of sunshine in a massage therapist's tunic. She never bears a grudge, never lets the world get her down. Even I, in all my surliness and silence, as the most infamous grouch in the city, can't seem to upset her for long—though god knows that's my biggest fear these days.

Four months in, she's got me conditioned like one of Pavlov's dogs. The elevator pings outside my office, announcing her arrival for our appointment, and already I'm calmer, the tension bleeding from my muscles. Already my chest feels looser, my lungs filling with air.

"Hey, Mr Katz." She pokes her head around my office door. Those freckles. Those *eyes*. "Ready to relax?"

Leaning back in my chair, I offer one of my standard awkward smiles. It still feels stiff and unnatural on my face, but it's worth the effort when Maisie lights up in response. "Definitely. Come in."

Lately, I've taken to clearing this whole afternoon. Maisie

comes at 3pm, but I like having at least an hour to prepare. To set up the table and towel; to prowl around my office like a caged tiger; to work myself into an agitated lather and then collapse behind my desk, breathing hard.

And once she's gone, I need time to recover too. The rest of the day is a write-off, because any time spent with Maisie leaves me raw—blundering through the world with my newfound feelings on my sleeve, not fit for public interaction.

So. Friday afternoons are now Maisie time.

The best part of the week.

"I walked past this churro cart on my way here." Maisie slips inside, locking the door behind her. The *thunk* of that lock always gives me a little thrill, though I know she doesn't mean anything by it. Still, it's a sign of trust. "It smelled amazing—all cinnamon sugar and hot dough. I nearly melted into a puddle of drool right there on the street."

"Then you should get churros on the way home."

She laughs, pleased by my answer. I resist the urge to punch the air. Has she always had me wrapped around her little finger, right from day one? It feels that way.

"Maybe you should come with me, Mr Katz. Treat yourself to something sweet." Maisie's eyes sparkle as she reaches the desk, slipping her tote bag off. "I'm sure you've earned it."

Christ. I know she doesn't really mean that invitation, but I'm so damn tempted. "Maybe I will."

Though let's be honest: there's only one sweet treat that I'm craving, and she's walking over to inspect the fish tank. Maisie's black hair is braided down her back today, and every time she moves her head, the end swings between her shoulder blades. Fish dance through the water, their scales sparkling in the light.

"So pretty," Maisie murmurs.

Yes. She is.

I stand, heart thumping. "Should I…?"

"Go ahead." A teasing smile over her shoulder. "I won't peek, I promise."

Ha. Part of me wishes she would, though I can't even articulate why. Maybe I don't want to be the only one driven half out of my mind by these appointments; maybe I want a hint, *any* hint, that I'm more than just a client. And a difficult one, at that.

My fingers move quickly, sliding my shirt buttons free. The fabric rustles as I shrug it off, draping it carefully over the back of my chair.

Cool air hits my bare skin. I'm flushed already, nipples pebbling, and my gut tightens as it always does when I strip for Maisie, peeling my clothes off with her in the room. And I know it's purely professional, I *know* she thinks nothing of it, but I can't help the hunger pounding through my veins.

Look at me.

Would she ever peek?

When she sees me undressed… does she like what she sees?

The massage table creaks beneath my weight. I drape the towel across my lap, glad for the heaviness of it—the way it hides my sins. "Ready."

She always takes one final breath before she turns around. Bracing herself? Trying not to seem repulsed?

Or maybe she's like me: trying desperately to remember that this is her work, that she wouldn't be here otherwise, that we shouldn't get any ideas.

A faint blush spreads over her cheeks as she walks over. I close my eyes and frown at the ceiling, pretending I didn't notice.

* * *

"You have scar tissue here." Maisie's voice is soft, twining around me where I lay bared on the table. Her thumbs probe at my shoulder, exploring the knotted flesh. It's tender, like poking an old bruise, but it's a good kind of pain. Everything with Maisie is a good kind of pain.

"Tore my rotator cuff in college."

"Playing sports?"

"Pitching baseball."

There's a long pause, like she's holding her breath. Then Maisie says, her voice higher pitched than before: "Baseball, huh? Did you wear those tight pants, Mr Katz?"

I grin into the darkness, eyes still closed. "For games." Her delighted laughter warms me down to my bones, and her fingertips scorch trails over my skin. Moving, always moving, goosebumps prickling in their path.

I'm haunted by these hands. For days after each appointment, I feel them ghosting over my body, tickling beneath my clothes.

"I can't imagine it," Maisie says. "You in those pants."

"No? Try harder."

Are we really flirting right now? I'm not imagining it, am I? Maisie's appreciative hum makes my heart lurch. No, I'm not imagining it. Fuck. "Okay, I see it now. I'm picturing it. Gosh, Mr Katz."

Definitely flirting. "Hudson."

"Hudson, then. Too bad about your shoulder." Maisie strokes down to my chest, kneading the thick muscle, and I fight to keep my breathing even. That heavy towel is working overtime, weighing down my rigid shaft. "Bet you looked great playing baseball."

"Yes, losing the pants was definitely the saddest part."

She lets out another peal of bright laughter. There's no better sound in the world.

"You know, this is what I like to see." Maisie's fingertip on my forehead makes me jolt, and I stiffen on the table. She presses gently between my eyebrows. "No frown."

As if by magic, the scowl settles back over my face. Maisie sighs and lifts her finger away, and we lapse into silence. I lie there with her hands on me, brooding and bemused and irritatingly turned on.

What did she mean by that? Does she find me too grumpy usually, the same as everyone else? Maybe she wishes I'd change—that I'd magically become a sunny, happy-go-lucky person. A completely different man.

But why flirt with me then? I am who I am. And Maisie gets by far the softest version of me, because everyone else gets the full ogre.

"Ready to turn over?" Maisie says at last, and she's all business again. No hint of the woman who teased me minutes ago.

"Yes." A chance to hide my disappointment—that's exactly what I need.

* * *

"You never touch me." Maisie blurts out the words at the end of our appointment, when she's wiping her oily hands on the towel. Her back is turned, and she stares into the fish tank while I dress. An angel fish floats a few inches from her nose, fins fluttering in the water.

I pause with my shirt half-fastened. "Excuse me?"

...Should I touch Maisie?

Could I touch her? Since when?

"Forget that. Sorry." Maisie's whole body seems to slump, and she stares down at the floor. The angel fish drifts away between the plants. "Can I turn around?"

What? Oh. "Yes," I rasp, doing the last few buttons up. Maisie spins around, her gray eyes snagging on the triangle of my bared chest before she looks away.

I could touch her? She'd really want that?

"I didn't realize I could. Touch you, I mean." Already, my heart knocks against my ribs, and the fish tank filter buzzes in my ears.

Where to start... cupping her cheek? Stroking her hair? I've dreamed about touching this woman so many times, spent so many fevered hours imagining her body pressed against mine. Her lips on my neck; my hands in her hair.

Where to begin?

"Yeah, you know. Like a handshake," Maisie says, staring past me at the wall. It's her turn to wear a scowl, and it looks as normal on her as a smile does on me. "Or a shoulder pat. Normal stuff."

My gut sinks.

Right. Obviously.

"I didn't mean to be rude." Crossing the room to her side, I revise my statement. "Not to you, anyway. To be honest, I don't really care about offending anyone else."

"I know." Her laugh is strained. "You're *the* Hudson Katz," she says, as if I might have forgotten my role as the most obnoxious man in the city.

162

It's strange standing beside her in this halfway state: pants and shirt on, feet bare. Usually, Maisie sees me all one way or the other. Why does this feel more vulnerable?

When I pat her shoulder, Maisie startles. Her chin jerks up, and she stares at me, wide-eyed. "Thank you for today," I offer. What else do normal people say to each other? "Good work."

Maisie splutters, but she doesn't move away. "Oh my god," she says at last. "You're like a robot learning to emote. That was wild."

Emote hardly seems to cover it. More like: I'm a robot whose cold electric circuits keep getting fried with my feelings for this woman. Burned to ash.

I nudge her arm. "How did I do?"

First a pat, now a nudge. If I'm truly allowed to touch her, even if only in these small, innocent ways, then she'd better buckle up. Maisie has opened the floodgates, because two touches will never be enough. Neither will two thousand.

"G-good." She smooths her hair, frazzled. Hands me the towel in a daze. "So... same time next week?"

When I can touch her again. Pat her shoulder, and maybe shake her hand. Game-changing.

"Yes. Same time next week."

If I survive without her that long.

Maisie

ᔐᕉᖓᕐ

An emergency appointment with Hudson Katz. Jeez. I hurry across the Midas Inc lobby, chewing on my bottom lip. Suited employees bustle all around, barking into phones and rustling papers, and I prod the elevator button, willing it to come fast.

What happened? Is Hudson okay? His assistant Carlton wouldn't give me any details, but our last appointment was only a few days ago. Maybe that shoulder injury flared up? Or maybe all this awful stress has finally gotten to him—felled him like a big, angry tree. God, I'd hate that.

"Come on, come on." I jab the elevator button again, impatient. My shoulders are tense, and I shift my weight from foot to foot. Long gone is my usual serenity. Normally I'm the island of calm in this lobby, but right now, I'm ready to tear out my hair.

When I got the call an hour ago, I canceled another appointment to be here. That's a cardinal sin for a massage therapist, but there was no way on this earth that I'd hear the words

'Hudson Katz' and 'emergency' in the same sentence and not come running. Oh god, what's wrong?

The elevator pings, and the doors slide open. It's already crammed with bodies, but I elbow my way on, ignoring the huffs and loud mutters. My forehead is sweaty, and I swipe it with my arm.

At floor nineteen, I realize: I forgot my massage therapist uniform. The sky blue tunic. My harried reflection in the elevator mirror, with pale cheeks and wild hair—she's in a daisy-patterned sundress. At least I remembered my tote! So unprofessional. Gah.

And it's a good thing Hudson keeps a massage table for me here, because no way would I have heaved that thing all the way on the subway, not while panicking and desperate to see him.

I hop from foot to foot, nerves fizzing. Could this freaking elevator go any slower? If it takes any longer, I'll be a skeleton in a sundress when we reach the top floor, slumped on the ground and covered in cobwebs.

Ping.

I hurtle out of the elevator onto the penthouse floor, banging my elbow against the nearest wall. Hudson's assistant stares at me from behind his desk, then calls my name as I tear past, but I don't slow down. *Can't* slow down, not until I've seen him.

I burst into Hudson's office, sweaty and red-faced and breathing hard. Hudson is on the phone. He lifts a finger to me, in the universal signal for: *be with you shortly.* Dark eyes rove over my sundress, and his deep voice rumbles on about quarterly figures.

Is he…?

Propping my hands on my hips, I suck in a strangled breath.

The office spins around me, and okay, I definitely need to do more cardio, but I focus on what matters: the healthy glow to Hudson's cheeks, his firm jaw and steady voice. His strong posture behind the desk, and the sheer vitality coming off him in waves.

He's fine! This asshole is totally fine!

Choking back a growl, I stomp to the massage table in the center of the room. The fish dart back and forth in their tank, as frazzled as my mood. My tote bag thumps against the table.

"Apologies," Hudson says, putting down the phone. I turn to face him with a glare. "Usually, I clear the whole afternoon for our appointments, but since this was so last minute—"

"An emergency," I interrupt, and wow, I don't sound like myself at all. My voice is clipped and taut, throbbing with anger. "Not 'last minute'. An emergency, your assistant said. *Where* is the emergency, Hudson?"

His mouth flattens. He sits up ramrod straight, and those dark eyes bore into me, crackling with challenge. Even though he's sitting down on the other side of the room, somehow it feels like he's looming over me. "I told Carlton it was urgent. Not an emergency."

Is he serious? I throw up my hands and lose all volume control, my voice bouncing around the penthouse office. "Hudson! How are those things any different? I thought you were hurt! I thought something serious had happened. I ran all the way here, and I freaking hate running!"

His mouth twitches; his scowl softens. How dare Hudson Katz discover his sense of humor *now*, when I've lost mine?

"You were worried about me," the Midas man says, and he sounds so pleased. His desk chair rattles over the floorboards, then he stands, shoulders suddenly taking up half the room.

He's in a deep blue suit today, so dark it's nearly black, with a white shirt unbuttoned at the collar.

No tie. That's new.

No! I will not gather details of this man, like a squirrel with a crush. I'm freaking *mad* at him. Ugh.

"I like the dress," Hudson says, rounding his desk. "Though of course I like your tunic too."

My teeth grind together, and my pulse races as he gets near. "What was so urgent, Mr Katz?"

The city's most famous grump stops right in front of me. His smile drains away, and he's suddenly solemn.

"I wanted to see you," he says quietly. "No emergency, I suppose, but it felt fairly urgent."

Thump. Thump. Thump. My heart slams against my ribs, and it's not from my sweaty run across the city, tote bag jostling my shoulder. Not from anger anymore. No, this is something else.

My dress is stuck to my back. My mouth is so dry. Wordlessly, I turn and dig in my bag for my water bottle, then crack the lid and swig.

Behind me, Hudson sighs. His suit rustles, and warmth tickles my shoulder. Out of the corner of my eye, I see his hand hovering above my skin, waiting for permission.

My chin jerks in a nod, throat still working as I drink, and Hudson's hand settles on my shoulder.

"I'm sorry," he says, and I can tell he means it this time. The pad of his thumb digs into my tense muscle, and I'm super glad he can't see my face, because my eyes practically cross.

Ooooh god. When was the last time *I* got a back rub? As in, not from my own hands? Can't even remember it. But here we are, with Hudson kneading both of my stiff shoulders now, his warmth against my back and his deep voice like velvet in my ear. "Forgive me, Maisie. I didn't think. I should have thought this through. But I'll make it up to you, I promise."

Well…

Okay yeah, he messed up. But if Hudson Katz was truly desperate to see me, if he wanted me here so badly he couldn't wait a few more days…

It's relatable. And so sweet it makes me giddy.

I breathe out, my chest loosening.

"Just text me next time. *You*, not Carlton."

Hudson makes a low noise, his big hands so firm against my shoulders. I've never resented the straps of my sundress before, but here they are cutting off two strips of skin-on-skin contact with my crush. Stupid straps.

"And… you don't need to make an appointment. Just say you want to hang out."

Hudson exhales. "Hang out?"

Honestly. He really is like a robot learning our human ways. I smile at the fish tank, swaying beneath his grip, and it's so sweet and sad and lovely. All the anger drains out of me in a rush, and my heart feels so full, because yes, this miscommunication was annoying—but what is there to *really* be mad about?

This grump wanted to see me. Urgently.

And I know the feeling. I know it well.

"Yeah. Hang out." Wetting my lips, I watch a tiny crab scuttle beneath a stone in the tank. "You know, like getting coffee together. Or drinks. Or going for a walk by the river. Or catching a movie, or cooking dinner together, or…"

Dates. I'm describing dates.

Because sure, you could do those things with friends, but when I picture them with Hudson, I picture kissing. Lots of kissing.

But does the Midas man kiss? Does he feel those kinds of feelings? Hudson's a celebrity, he features on Hottest Bachelor lists and gets hounded for gossip mags, but he's never been seen with a date. Believe me, I've checked.

And sure, his hands are moving greedily over my bare shoulders right now, but he's not roaming further south. Not trying to slip beneath the fabric of my dress, or press his body against my back.

Am I alone in this? We have a connection, sure. That's undeniable. But does he want me the same way I want him?

Slowly, I screw the water bottle cap back on and place it next to my tote bag.

Okay. Okay. Time to be brave.

I suck in a deep breath, then say, "You're good at that." He is, too. My shoulders feel looser already, less achy. Other parts of me are throbbing like hell, but that's a separate problem. "So... here's an idea. A way for you to make things up to me. Only if you want to, obviously, and really I'm already over it, so if you don't like this idea you definitely shouldn't agree—"

"You're babbling."

I roll my eyes. Awesome.

Hudson squeezes my shoulders. "Tell me your idea."

Here goes. "Role reversal," I whisper, then squeak as he leans in closer. His spicy clean-man scent fills my nose.

"Say it again," he commands. "At a normal volume."

"Role reversal," I say, louder this time. My cheeks are blazing hot. "I'm definitely the more stressed party right now, Hudson Katz. And you're nailing this back rub. So if you're up for it..." I trail off, horrified at myself.

Wait. What am I suggesting? What am I thinking? This is

the kind of request you make of your boyfriend, not a client. I don't go to my dentist, then clean *his* teeth. How did I ever think this might be okay?

It's that girls' night, putting ideas in my head. Those mojito-fueled confessions, and the way Priya and Fliss encouraged me. They spurred me on, made me think I could actually date this man. They legitimized my crush, and now I've stepped way out of line.

"Yes," Hudson says. The floor drops out beneath me. His hands lift away, and when I peek back over my shoulder, he's turned around to let me get undressed.

Get. Undressed.

So that my client can massage *me*. Aah!

"This is nuts," I say, and I wholly mean it, but I'm also sliding the dress straps off my shoulders. The girls will lose their minds when I tell them how reckless I've been. Alarm bells blare in my head, but like a lovesick idiot, I keep going.

Because I need to know—need to see if Hudson wants me the same way. Need to see if he'll take this golden opportunity to kiss me.

"I won't hurt you," Hudson says, as if that's what I'm worried about. "I know to avoid the spine. And I'll be gentle."

"Not too gentle, I hope."

The Midas man splutters out a cough, and I'm savagely glad, my dress whooshing past my thighs to puddle around my feet. The cool air sends goosebumps prickling over my skin.

Yes, I'm setting my whole career on fire right now, but I don't care, okay? I don't care.

I need answers. And his hands on my body.

Else I'll go mad.

Hudson

✦

I f it weren't for the feedback from all my senses, I'd think this was a dream. After all, I've pictured a moment like this plenty of times over the last four months.

Maisie's bare body is stretched out on her front on the massage table, her hands pillowed beneath her head. All that creamy skin and those freckles are on full display. There's a mole near her hip, and dimples at the base of her spine, and I swallow at the delicate shift of her shoulder blades as she fidgets to get comfortable. Her dark hair is thrown in a messy bun.

Yeah. My money would definitely be on *dream*. Except the fish tank filter has never hummed in the background in my dreams; the room has never been this cool; Carlton's muffled voice has never floated through the wall as he talks on the phone.

"One moment," I say. My steps echo across the office, and Carlton's voice gets louder as I near the door. I spin the lock, throat tight, and glance back at Maisie. "Is this alright?"

We can leave it unlocked if she prefers, but if Carlton bursts in here and sees Maisie undressed, I'll have to burn his whole life down and chase him out of the city. And I hate hiring new assistants, so that's not ideal.

She nods, her cheek squished against her hand. "It's alright."

So much trust in one day. It presses on my chest—makes it harder to breathe.

I *cannot* screw this up. I'll go mad.

But already, the sight of Maisie's sundress puddled on the floor by the table makes me want to bellow and sprint around the block. My hands ball into fists.

Need to touch her.

Stroke her.

Need to bury my face against her shoulder blades, and feel each tiny shift as she draws breath. Need to drag Maisie's most intimate scents into my lungs, and sink my teeth into the swell of her ass, currently hidden beneath that white towel.

"The oil is in my bag."

Right: a massage. I'm giving her a massage. This is not an access–all–areas pass, and maybe that's the real punishment. The real way I'm to atone for my sins.

Taunting me with what I'll never have. Harsh but fair.

Her belongings rattle together as I search through the bag. A hairbrush, a compact mirror, a notepad, a pen. A tin of breath mints and a tube of lipstick that I've never seen Maisie wear. It's so *red*. How would her lips look, stained this shade of crimson and wrapped around my cock?

Christ. Not helping.

My heart thumps faster as I hold up the oil at last, cracking open the lid. It pools in my palm, and I place the bottle down then rub my hands together, warming the oil like Maisie always

172

does. It smells like orange blossoms.

Maisie bites her lip as I move closer. Her gray eyes track my movements, widening as they stare up at me.

I pause, both palms hovering over her bare back. "Ready? It's not too late to change your mind." Though if she says no, I'll die.

Maisie's eyes flutter closed. "No," she says. "I'm ready."

And…

Her heat tickles my palms before I reach her skin. Her back rises and falls as she breathes faster, squirming on the massage table. That white towel rustles as she shifts, and my throat is too tight to speak, and when my hands finally make contact—

I choke back a groan.

So warm. So soft. Maisie is so *alive*, her heartbeat thumping against my roving fingers, her body never one hundred percent still. An escaped strand of dark hair tickles my wrist, and I shake my head silently, stroking both hands along her shoulders.

There are two pink lines where her sundress straps dug in. I knead them with my thumbs, wishing I could smooth them away.

All her aches and pains; all her stresses and cares. I'd dedicate my life to fixing them, if she'd only let me. So much for the grumpy, evil Midas man.

Instead, I have this: an unknown amount of time with my hands on her body. Perhaps two minutes, perhaps an hour. Depends when Maisie gets tired of torturing me, I suppose. Punishing me for my 'emergency' appointment.

Maisie shifts and chews her lip. "You can press a little harder," she whispers.

Gritting my teeth, I do as she says, keeping my hips a careful inch away from the table. No need for Maisie to know that her words leave me harder than granite. She's set the terms—a massage, nothing more—and I'll abide by them, even if it kills me.

After months of watching this woman out of the corner of my eye, I thought I knew all her quirks and features. I already spotted the scar on the back of her left elbow; already memorized the soft, curling hairs at the back of her neck. But now, with my hands coasting over her body, finally free to look my fill, it's clear my explorations have barely begun.

Is she ticklish anywhere?

Are there freckles on her ass?

How would she fit, tucked against the side of my body? Stretched out together in my bed on a lazy Sunday morning, reading the paper together. Doing the crossword.

Maisie hums, and my gut twists in response. Back to reality. "Feels really good," she mumbles, eyes still closed. I stroke down to her lower back, rubbing small circles with my thumbs—and when Maisie bites her lip, I get the feeling that she's waiting for something. Hoping for something. Testing me somehow, but why? What does she want? What am I missing, damn it?

"Should I do your front?" I ask, and Christ, the second the question is out, I want to charge across the office and slam my head against the fish tank. There's only one towel, and Maisie's not wearing a bra. It's a ridiculous offer.

But: "Sure," Maisie murmurs, and I turn to stone as she rolls over, the pink beads of her nipples coming into view. Her bun squishes to one side beneath her head, and her breasts are small and perfect—less than a handful. Just how I've shamelessly, hopelessly pictured them all these months.

"Ngh," I say.

Maisie's mouth twitches, but she keeps her eyes closed. "Keep going, Mr Katz."

Fuck. Keep going? Touch her—touch her like *this*, her nipples peaked, a flush creeping up her neck? With her breath coming faster and that white towel slipping down her hips?

This. Is. Torture.

"I don't know the rules," I manage to say, kneading her shoulders again with shaky fingers. Her shoulders, where it is safe. PG land. "Where can I...?"

Maisie shrugs, and the movement slips my thumbs into the dips beneath her collarbone. Her pulse thrums against my touch. "Wherever you like."

Hm. Is there a hidden camera in this room? A TV crew about to jump out and yell "GOTCHA!"? Is this some kind of twisted joke?

"Wherever I like," I repeat, testing out the words. Nope. Definitely a trap. "And if I do something you don't want..."

"Then I'll tell you." Maisie's smile is so sweet, even with her eyes closed. There's no frown in her forehead. She's peaceful while I loom over her, losing my mind.

Well, then.

There are a million things I want to do to her right now, but I settle for letting my hands drift lower, leaving the safe harbor of her shoulders. Her breasts are soft compared to her muscles and bones, and I cup them guiltily, feeling like a criminal. Ready for her to scream and launch off the table, slapping me across the face. Ready for the punchline.

But Maisie hums, smiling wider. She shifts, arching her back, and presses more firmly into my hands.

Jesus. She's not... she's not messing with me?

175

"You really like this?" My thumbs rub her nipples, and my mouth is so dry. Want to suck on them. Want to *bite*.

"From you," Maisie says, still squirming, and that flush has reached her cheeks. "I really like this from you, Hudson Katz."

Fuck. My face is locked in my usual scowl, and my pulse throbs in my ears as I cup and knead her breasts. Too good to be true.

The floor creaks as I move along the massage table. The white towel rustles in my grip, and I lift it an inch, pausing there.

"Go on," Maisie says. The fabric drags slowly to one side, dropping to the floor with a soft thump.

Her thighs part.

Christ.

And there's still so much more I want to do, so many places I want to touch and tease and taste, but Maisie draws her legs wider, showing me the center of the goddamn universe, and it's slick and pink and swollen for me already, her hips lifting as she lets out a sigh.

"I've got you." I press on her hip, weighing her back down. Nudge her thighs even wider with the other hand. "Do you want to feel good, sweetheart? Is that what this is about?"

Maisie's breath catches as she nods. Small fingers have found my belt loop, hooking through the fabric, keeping me anchored as though I might run.

Hardly.

The angle is awkward, my neck already twinging as I lean over the side of the massage table, Maisie's knee pressing against my stomach. But all that fades away when I breathe in a lungful of her salty musk; when I feel her warmth down here, the hint of moisture in the air. My temples throb.

Somewhere over my head, somewhere on another planet, fish float between the green tendrils of water plants, their scales sparkling. Carlton drones into a distant phone, his voice muffled.

That isn't real. *This* is.

Maisie's moan is agonized when I lick her, but she lifts her hips again, demanding more. Her free hand grips the table above her head, and her posture is so sensual, so obscene, her nipples pointing at the ceiling. This is a whole new angle to view her from—her dips and swells, her secret topography—and my eyes are dry from refusing to blink.

Don't want to miss a single second of this.

Hot. Wet. I work her with my tongue. Lick and suck and nibble, roaming over every inch, tasting inside her and torturing her clit. When I press one finger inside her then two, pumping in and out, knuckles shiny, I marvel at the fierce way she grips me.

Yeah, she's *seriously* tight. A belated suspicion tickles my brain.

"Have you ever done this before, Maisie?"

"N-no."

My heart beats hard enough to crack a rib. "Me neither."

Why would I have? No one else interests me the way Maisie does. No one else brings out my softer side, and no one else would dare challenge me to this game of chicken. We live in a world of time-wasting idiots, we're surrounded on all sides, and Maisie is the only person I have ever wanted to spend time with.

Spend time with. Such a weak phrase for the things I feel for this woman. Spend time with her? I want the rest of her goddamn life. Want to see her walk toward me in a wedding dress, and want to watch her gorgeous body swell with my baby. Make that babies, plural.

Yeah, sure. We can *spend time.*

But this will have to be enough. She hasn't asked for any of that—only my mouth and hands on her body. Her sighs fills my ears.

And if Maisie wants pleasure… I'll give her pleasure. Bowing my head, I snarl into her slit, bitterness warring with my primal satisfaction at her salty-sweet taste. I want so much more from her, and it's already too much to bear.

Don't know how much time passes—could be minutes, could be hours. Don't care. I'll die down here. I'll die happy.

Maybe that would be preferable. Better to go out on a high than to resurface and go back to *normal.* Back to my cold, empty life; my strange envy for those fish with their peaceful existence. Hours and weeks and months of yearning for Maisie.

Will she still massage me after this?

What if she balks—finds it all too weird? What if I'm ruining everything right now?

Too late. My fingers are shiny with the evidence of how *too late* it is. Her taste is on my lips and tongue; her rasping breaths echo around my brain. At some point, Maisie plunged one hand into my hair, and now she's tugging, twisting, a sweet pain prickling over my scalp.

"Oh! Hudson—"

I growl and clamp my lips around her clit, sucking hard. My fingers crook inside her, her inner muscles squeezing tight, and it's like I've pressed a secret button, because—

Maisie detonates.

She shakes and trembles. Gasps and moans. Yanks my hair

hard enough that moisture stings in my eyes. Her whole body is caught up in the storm, pleasure wracking her in waves, and I suck her through all of it, jaw aching.

Beside the table, I'm so hard it hurts. When I press my hips against the padded edge, it gives no relief—only makes my gut twist tighter.

"Oh," Maisie says at last, so hoarse it's like she's been screaming at a rock concert. "Oh, god." She collapses in a sweaty heap, nudging my head away. "Oh, god, stop. Please stop. You're going to kill me."

In a good way? My back aches like hell as I straighten up, fiery pain crackling across the muscles, and the irony is not lost on me. This is the first massage appointment where I'll go home in worse shape than when we started.

Worth it.

I wipe my mouth on my forearm. Maisie watches the movement, her eyes heavy-lidded. She's still breathing hard, still clinging to my belt loop with one hand, and her chest is one big blush.

"Was that alright?" I demand.

Maisie's laugh is strangled. "Better than alright."

…Okay. That's good.

Shoulders dropping, I scrub one hand over my face. Every breath I draw is laced with her scent. Her taste is seared on my tongue. Was this a one-off thing? Should have asked before we started, because if I never get to do that again, I'll be ruined for life.

"Can't wait 'til Friday," Maisie jokes weakly, sitting up with a groan. She rolls her neck, like she's aching too. "I'm gonna need our appointment more than you."

Guess that answers my question. Whatever this is, it can

happen again.

By appointment only.

Maisie

"Hudson Katz *again?*" Fliss gapes at me from our sofa, where she sits with both legs draped over her boss-turned-boyfriend, Sebastian. They've paused their movie while I bustle around the living room, snatching up my keys and phone and wallet and every other trinket I own, blindly stuffing it all in my tote bag. I'm in my blue massage therapist's tunic, and it's getting dark outside.

"*The* Hudson Katz?" Sebastian says.

Fluss nods, staring at me over Rusty's moth-eaten head. Her cat is snuggled against her chest, shooting smug looks at his human rival. "Isn't it a bit late? Since when do you do evening appointments?"

Since Hudson and I started hooking up in his office every chance we got. Since his appointments suddenly became daily instead of weekly. Since every hour I spend away from that man makes the ache inside me grow worse.

Sometimes Hudson massages me, then ends the session with his head between my legs, our bodies lit only by the glow of the

181

fish tank. Sometimes I massage *him*, then peel the towel away and suck on his thick shaft like it's the world's most delicious lollipop. Not the happy ending I was hoping for with Hudson Katz, but one I'm addicted to nonetheless.

Pathetic? Hell yes. A blow to my bruised heart? Every time.

But I don't care. When it comes to the Midas man, I'll take whatever I can get.

"He tore his rotator cuff in college," I say, as though that explains the sudden barrage of appointments.

Sebastian's eyebrow raises. "Ah, yes. It's time sensitive, then."

Fliss snorts, and I give them both the stink eye as I shove an umbrella in my bag. Out of everyone in this room, only Rusty gets me. My jacket sleeve is inside out, and I huff as I wrestle it on, trying to punch my way through.

"Maisie," Fliss says, more gently this time. I brace myself and pause, breathing hard. "Is he still… paying you? For this?"

Shame swarms my insides.

Oh god, she knows. She knows what I'm doing. Is it that obvious? Does Priya know too?

"I'm not judging!" Fliss says quickly, petting Rusty in nervous strokes until he meows and lashes his tail. "You know I'll support you no matter what, and Priya will too. But I thought you really liked him. Are you sure this is what you want?"

Is it? I bite my lip, jacket half on.

No. Not even close.

Hudson's breath against my belly button, his teeth scraping my nipple, his muscles quaking under my palms—yes. I want that.

But the scheduling? The payment for something I desperately want to do for free? The cold, hollow feeling I get walking home afterward? The non-stop *longing*, blistering my chest from the inside, demanding that I stay with Hudson for more than an hour at a time, and that he kiss my lips for once?

No. This hurts so much.

My chin wobbles. Fliss lunges off the sofa, dumping Rusty on Sebastian's lap, ignoring both sets of protests.

Her arms wrap around me, and I hug her back, clinging and tragic.

"It's my fault," I wail, the words muffled by her pink-streaked hair. "I started us on this path, and maybe if I hadn't, he'd have asked me out for real. But why would he ever want to date me now? He's getting everything with no strings attached, and there's no way Hudson would ever want the messier version. He hates feelings."

"Have you asked him?" Sebastian says quietly. His deep voice cuts through the room.

Huh. Kind of forgot my roommate's boyfriend was even there. "No," I say, still hugging Fliss. Her yellow pinstripe pajamas crinkle in my grip, and I'm ruining their movie night, but whatever. There is a limit to how much guilt I can feel in one go, and I'm maxed out.

"You should ask him," Sebastian says, like it's truly that simple. "Some men want the mess. They would rather have something real."

And I scoff, but when Fliss and I pull apart, she smiles at her boyfriend, all misty-eyed. "Sebastian tried to pay me for our first weekend together," she says, glancing back at me. "Remember? He tried to give me overtime, and I had to tell him no. They're idiots, Maisie."

And her boss rolls his eyes, but he's so fond when he looks at her. The love beams out of his eyes, focused into lasers by those nerdy glasses.

Then Rusty steps on his crotch, and he winces. Moment over.

"I should ask him," I say, rehearsing the thought out loud.

"Yes!" Fliss pumps the air. "You should totally just *ask* him. Tonight! Then video chat us and tell us how it goes."

"Fully clothed," Sebastian adds quickly.

Fliss sticks out her tongue. "Prude."

I leave them there, bathed in the glow of their happiness, and step out into the cool night. My tote bag weighs down my shoulder, crammed full of god only knows what, but as I walk down the street... for the first time in weeks, my steps are light.

* * *

Ask him.

Just ask him.

Ask Hudson how he feels.

The instructions play on a loop in my brain, keeping time with my steps. I march to their beat along the subway platform, and they repeat over and over as I sway in place on the train.

I should ask him. I *will* ask him. How hard could it be? And what exactly am I risking? My favorite client, yes. My daily hook up and my pride. Sure.

And my heart.

Ugh.

The train rattles through the stone warren beneath the city, and I cling, grim-faced, to my pole, searching for the right words to say. The magic words that will lead to my *real* happy ending.

But as I step off the train, I've got nothing. Just an aching shoulder from carrying my bag, and the early rumblings of a headache.

It's getting late, stars prickling through the night sky over-head, but the financial district still clamors with life. Half the office windows are lit up in their skyscrapers—money never sleeps, I guess—and the streets bustle with tourists and sellers.

One rickety table groans under the weight of key chains, dusty shot glasses, and baseball caps. The next has two chairs and a board covered in sharpie sketches, with a slumped caricaturist buried in her jacket, napping as people stream past.

Cars rumble in the road. Lights turn red, then green, then back.

I hover outside the Midas Inc skyscraper, my belly squirming with nerves.

What if he says no? What if this is all Hudson ever wants from me?

And what if he gets bored of even *this* soon? Crap. My chest splinters at the mere thought. Okay, gotta keep moving.

It's cool in the Midas Inc lobby. The lights are bright, the floor shiny, and even though the working day ended hours ago, I have plenty of company in the elevator. Hudson's employees stream in and out, the elevator stuttering through the floors, all talking on their phones or tapping out an email, moving with certainty and purpose.

Maybe I should throw myself into my career, like these folks. Get super intense about massage. Kind of defeats the point, but if Hudson doesn't want me... maybe that's how I'll cope.

Ping.

For once, I'm reluctant to step onto the top floor. The doors swoosh closed behind me, the elevator already humming down to pick up someone new, and part of me wants to pound on the metal doors and beg for it to come back and pick me up. I force myself forward instead.

Carlton's desk stands empty—a neat, silent sentinel. My fingertips brush the wood as I walk past. *Wish me luck.*

Hudson's office door is open. He stands by the window, arms folded, gazing out at the lit-up city skyline.

"Hey," I say softly, leaning in the doorway.

He turns and smiles, arms dropping to his sides. I swear, every time this man smiles at me, the expression looks a little more comfortable on his face. More at home. More natural. "Maisie. Hello."

The massage table is already set up, complete with the folded white towel, even though that kind of shyness is a distant memory. We've seen every inch of each other. We've felt each other come.

But we'll go through this whole dance anyway. We'll pretend this is a normal appointment—nothing to see here, folks. No broken rules, and no sticky feelings.

"Ready?" Hudson asks, strolling toward the table. His fingers are deft, flicking his shirt buttons open one by one, the triangle of his bared golden chest getting wider. The valleys of his muscles are shadowed.

His turn tonight. My mouth waters just thinking about it— my hands on his body, the heavy weight of him on my tongue, his clean, masculine scent in my lungs—but as I join him by the table, I hold up a palm. "Wait. Wait a second. I need to ask you something first."

Hudson leans against the table and waits, so calm. Dark eyes rove over my body, my face, the pinch between my eyebrows.

"Do you…"

The fish tank hums by the wall, the glow tinting the room blue. Shapes drift between the plants, pale as tiny ghosts under their night light.

I clear my throat and try again. "Hudson, do you... have you ever..."

The words die on my tongue, and Hudson raises an eyebrow. Heat crawls up my neck. This is a famously impatient man, and I'm wasting his time.

Ugh. Screw this. "Is your shoulder better?" I blurt.

Hudson frowns. "It's fine." He waits, but when it becomes clear that I'm done chewing on my own tongue, he starts flicking his shirt buttons open again, his movements slow.

He stops halfway down his abs. His beautiful, beautiful abs. "Would you rather have a turn tonight? Or would you rather reschedule? You don't seem..."

What don't I seem?

Happy? Mellow? *Sane?*

Hahahahaha.

"I'm fine," I say, echoing his words. The heel of my hand digs into my eye. "Just tired. But let's do this," I add when Hudson's frown deepens. "Let's do this. I want to."

Every day for the rest of my life, I want to do this. That's the whole freaking problem, but Hudson still moves extra slowly to undo his final buttons, watching me the whole time. "Alright."

The fabric slips from his shoulders, and all that sculpted perfection comes into view, tinted by the blue light from the tank.

I can't help myself. My body moves with a mind of its own, stepping between the Midas man's thighs where he leans against the table. My palms spread over his strong chest, and I press a kiss right over his heart.

Hudson grunts like I punched him in the stomach.

"S-sorry." Way too late, I stumble back, cheeks on fire. Because we don't do that—we don't casually touch and kiss. We're not lovers, we're whatever *this* is. A calendar-scheduled tryst.

But Hudson catches my wrist and tugs me back in close, back to where his heat and scent make me reckless. He cups the back of my neck, so gentle my stomach hurts.

"Do that again," Hudson says.

I take a shuddering breath, then press a second kiss over his heart.

And Hudson groans like I've done something pornographic, not given him a chaste peck on the chest. His grip tightens, and the massage table creaks as he shifts his weight.

"Again."

I kiss the hollow of his throat this time, then work my way left along his collarbone, all the way to his shoulder, then do the same on the other side. And Hudson keeps still, his body thrumming with tension. The hand on my neck slides into my hair.

"Again."

Back to the hollow of his throat. My tongue flicks out, tasting the salt on his skin, then I kiss my way up Hudson Katz's neck.

"Maisie," he breathes. I rock onto my tiptoes, but I can't quite reach his mouth. "Maisie," he says again.

So I grip his shoulders and climb onto the table, knees on either side of Hudson's hips. It creaks angrily under the lopsided strain, metal scraping, but I don't care.

Not when two big hands find my ass, boosting me higher. Holding me close. Not when my arms are around his neck, and his breath is on my cheek, and somehow even though we've *tasted* each other, we've never been close like this before.

"What were you going to ask me?" Hudson demands, challenge sparking in his dark eyes. "Tell me the truth this time, you little coward."

Um, excuse me? I twist his nipple, and Hudson chokes out a curse. He swats my ass, the heat prickling under my clothes.

"Why should I be the vulnerable one?" I glare from inches away, so intoxicated at being in his arms—and so freaking irritated. "I did that last time, you big jerk. When are you gonna take one for the team?"

Hudson straightens, affronted. "I didn't think you'd want that. Didn't want to scare you off. If I'd known—"

"You *can't* know, dummy. That's why it's so vulnerable. That's why it sucks."

Hudson frowns at me. A muscle ticks in his jaw. I wait, my stomach tangled in one giant knot.

Am I asking too much? Risking it all? With an ordinary man, maybe a demand like that could work: a man like Fliss has, like Sebastian, with his nerdy glasses and his pajama pants and the way he cooks her pancakes with bacon and syrup on Sunday mornings.

I know Fliss would probably not describe the love of her life as 'ordinary'. But no one ever fled in tears from Sebastian, you know? He's stern and serious sometimes, but he's so *reasonable*.

Hudson Katz is not reasonable. Hudson Katz is a thunder-cloud in a tailored suit, and his underlings scurry from him in the halls, whispering about weather warnings. Hudson Katz is the stuff of legend.

"Maisie…" He says my name so begrudgingly. Like he's being held at gunpoint, and god, who dreams of a confession like this? No one, that's who.

I tap his shoulder, all my earlier hopes going sour. "Okay, put me down."

"What?" Strong arms grip me tighter, and Hudson scowls from three inches away. "No, not yet. I'm not done."

"Hudson."

"*Maisie.* Let me think, will you?" He jostles me against his chest, like he wants to oh-so-gently shake some sense into me. "You just set the highest stakes of my whole fucking life, and I need a minute. I need to get this right."

My lips press together, and my bruised heart lifts. The highest stakes? The highest in his whole life?

Maybe that's enough. Maybe that says it all. Maybe we're both clueless but desperately, hopelessly stuck on each other.

I kiss the tip of his nose. "I love you."

Hudson's glare is thunderous, even as his heart beats faster against my front, so strong I feel it even through my tunic. "I was going to say it first, Maisie."

Aah!

I shrug, fighting a grin. "Too slow."

And his snarl, his heat, the teeth on my throat, the rough hand in my hair… it's perfect. The best confession I could have wished for.

"I love you," Hudson grits out, like he's mad about it, but I know better. He's mad that I said it first. That I threw down the gauntlet, then changed my mind and picked it up myself. It pains him. "I love you so fucking much. You're *mine*, Maisie, and I'm going to keep you forever. Do you understand?"

"Uh-huh." Can't stop grinning as he turns us around and sets me on the massage table, shoving the towel onto the floor. My tunic rucks up around my hips, already creased from climbing all over my client, and—

No. Not my client.

My boyfriend? Lover?

The demon in a suit that bargained for my soul?

Don't care. It's all details, because Hudson is right. I'm his, and he's mine, and I remind him of that fact with ten red lines scored down his chest with my fingernails, the sides of his shirt brushing my wrists. He hisses, yanking my leggings and underwear down my hips, stripping me from the waist down and tossing it all into a shadowed corner.

"I love you," he says again, and he's still pissed, jaw flexing. He shoves my thighs apart, crowding close—and *damn*, I love being manhandled by Hudson Katz. I'm giddy, a rapid pulse thudding between my thighs, already slick with how much I want him. "You don't know what you've started, Maisie. You don't know what you've unleashed. You think I love you in that petty, pedestrian way that every other asshole in this city feels?" His belt clinks. Hudson notches at my entrance, and his dark eyes glitter down at me. "You're wrong."

A stinging sensation. *Pressure*. My body trembles.

"Let me in," Hudson commands. He bends down and sucks a bruise on my throat, and I cling to his open shirt. "Maisie, let me in. Feel what you've done."

My voice is shaky in the darkened office. "It's not that simple. You're really *big*, okay, and I've never done this before. It's not an 'open sesame' deal."

And all I meant was that I needed to go slow, to take a moment to adjust, but Hudson crashes to his knees and buries his face against my slit. With both hands squeezing my thighs, it's savage the way he licks me, sucks me, nips with his teeth. I wheeze for breath, clinging to his thick, dark hair.

191

"Oh my god." I yank on the strands, but he ignores me, even when my hips jerk and I choke out a wail. "Hudson! Oh my *god*."

You know, we've done this before. Plenty of times by now, because there seems to be some secret ingredient between my legs that the Midas man is always hungry for. But it's never felt like *this*, like being eaten alive, and when I come, it's in record time.

I barely recognize the sound of my own voice. I'm *ragged*. "Oh. Oh, shit."

Then Hudson looms above me once more, scowling as he lines up again. "That was no hardship," he says, and yeah, I felt his enthusiasm in every lash of his tongue, in the vibration of every growl, "but now you will let me in. I need in, Maisie."

My shaking legs move wider. I'm desperate for this too.

Hudson grunts in approval, then presses forward again.

Hudson

❧

C an this be real? Could I get this lucky? How do I know I'm not slumped over my desk at 3pm on a rainy Tuesday, passed out from exhaustion as emails ping one after another into my inbox?

It's too good to be true. *Maisie* is too good to be true, and getting to touch her… taste her…

With our new routine over the last few weeks, I thought I'd struck gold. Thought I'd won the lottery, and that I should be grateful for every second with her, even if it killed me to let her go after every appointment. Shouldn't let myself get greedy.

Now I see the truth: those encounters were a shadow of this. A weak imitation, cartoonish and wrong, like the sloppy caricatures that hack artist draws on the sidewalk near this building.

This time, our hearts thunder in sync. This time, I finally press inside, stretching Maisie's slick channel—filling her up and feeling her pulse tap against my shaft.

"Oh," she says, eyelids fluttering.

Yes. *Oh.*

My grip is harsh on her hips, my face set in a scowl. Anyone else would probably cower from me, but Maisie yanks me closer, burying her face in my neck. I need her so badly, it turns me feral. Makes me forget how to speak, how to be gentle, how to do anything except press inside her, invading inch by inch, panting hot against her hair.

"Mine," I grit out, the only word left in my vocabulary. "Mine."

Maisie whimpers, her body sucking me deeper. I can't breathe.

When I bottom out, when our bodies are sealed as tight as they can go, I rub my face against her silky black hair. My stubble rasps against the strands, barely audible over the fish tank hum and the faint rumble of traffic and our strained breaths.

I've never done this before. Never felt the urge.

Now I may never stop.

Want to pound this woman until she sobs for relief, clinging to my shoulders; want to work her into a sweaty mess again and again and again.

"Mean face," Maisie whispers, leaning back in my arms and smoothing the pinch of my eyebrows with her thumb. "Don't you like it, Mr Katz?"

"No, I do." Obviously. "But it's too good. So good I'm losing my mind, and I'm pissed about it."

Maisie snorts and nibbles my chin, clearly delighted with my answer. "Temper, temper."

My heart is working overtime, racing like I've just run ten miles. And my fingers shake, but when I take a fistful of her hair, wrapping the strands around my palm—I'm still gentle.

That's a relief. Beneath these dark, hungry eddies, I'm still careful with her. My Maisie.

"Need to fuck you," I mutter, and this feels like a confession too, just as vulnerable as earlier. The Midas man is out of control, and what if that puts her off? What if she liked me icy and unreachable, like my legend says? "I'll try to make it good. But I—if I don't fuck you soon, and hard—"

"Do it," Maisie interrupts, the massage table creaking as she shifts her ass closer. I throb inside her. "I've been waiting for so long, Hudson. Please, do it."

My teeth grind as I draw back.

I slam forward, and Maisie hiccups a moan.

We start slow then build speed, sweat dripping, the table rattling like it's caught in an earthquake. Fish flit back and forth in the tank, their scales flashing in the edge of my vision.

She's so tight and wet and hot. Knees clamped around my waist, her head lolling from my grip in her hair; lips parted and eyes hazy.

Maisie watches me from beneath heavy lids as I pound into her, working out months and months of clawing hunger in one go. She bites her lip against a cry.

"No more appointments," I grind out, moisture trickling down my spin, muscles aching as I grip her, clasp her, shove my way deeper. "No more goddamn calendar reminders. Say it, Maisie." A little shake. "You'll wake up in my bed and kneel for me in the shower. You'll introduce me to your friends. You'll take me to your bedroom and stretch out for me on your mattress and let me lick you until you scream."

"I have roommates," Maisie gasps, but her eyes are sparkling, her cheeks flushed. Her hips rock forward with each thrust, meeting me, coaxing me deep. "There'll be no screaming."

I blink sweat from my eyes. "We'll see."

And we slam together in a torturous rhythm. When I cram a hand between us, finding her clit with my thumb, Maisie arches like a drawn bowstring.

Such a calm, gentle girl—but with me, she's a firecracker.

"Come for me." The air's muggy with our sweat. Our breaths. The massage table is about to rattle apart, and pleasure stabs me in the gut, then twists the blade. Won't last much longer. My thumb rubs back and forth. "Come for me."

"It's not... that... easy..." Maisie trails off with a shaky breath, suddenly curling forward. Her forehead thumps against my collarbone, and I keep rubbing, thrusting, driving her higher and higher.

She's so perfect.

So perfect it hurts.

And when Maisie's teeth dig into my shoulder, when she cries out into my unbuttoned shirt—I know I've got her. Her body locks up, trembling and jerking, pulsing tighter around my shaft. On and on, it strangles me.

There.

She's mine. Claimed.

Thank god.

Wedging myself deep, I press her ass close—and let go with a groan. Fill her with spurt after spurt of wet warmth, as sparks crackle up my spine.

It's primal, filling her up like this. So necessary.

And it *aches.* Feels like I've been kicked in the gut.

"Oh my god," Maisie mumbles eventually, clinging to my shoulders. She draws back and glances down between us, expression hazy. "Does this table wipe down?"

That's what she's worried about? After we just cracked our chests wide open; after I went inside her bare? *That's* her biggest worry? Maybe I've done some things right after all.

For the first time in recent memory, I throw back my head and laugh.

* * *

Two years later

I find my wife on the roof terrace, slathering sunscreen on her pale limbs. A sky blue bikini covers her secret places—but barely. Thank god our rooftop is high and sheltered, away from prying eyes.

"Want a hand?"

Maisie startles at the sound of my voice, then beams as I stroll closer. With my hands in my pockets, shirt sleeves rolled, I'm done working for the day. Who in his right mind would work late and miss *this*, with Maisie's bare, freckled skin on display, her legs stretched out in the afternoon sunshine?

It's late summer but the heat is holding on, baking the sidewalk down below. The city is lazy and loose. I used to hate this time of year, used to rail against how everyone took their eyes off the ball, but look at me now.

I have new priorities. Obviously.

There's Maisie, first and foremost, the center of my galaxy—and now the bump curving her small belly.

That bump is slathered with sunscreen, dotted with freckles. So perfect. I sink on to the empty sun lounger at my wife's side, pluck the bottle out of her hands and squeeze a dollop of sunscreen into my palm.

"Hello, love."

I start at her feet and work my way up, rubbing and teasing as I go. Maisie melts back against the lounger with a sigh, her head pillowed on a pink towel, happy to put me in charge.

We have a lot of practice with this. Our main language has always been touch—it's how we declare our love and devotion, over and over again. How we renew our promises each day. Even from the very first time we met, our bodies understood what took our minds a while longer.

"Don't stay in the sun for too long," I warn, kneading her right thigh.

"Bossy," Maisie says, her lips curving in a smile.

She likes it. Likes me fussing over her, making sure she's well fed and hydrated and gets plenty of sleep. Plenty of other things, too. Speaking of which…

I hook her bikini, dragging it down over her hips. Maisie lifts her ass to help, then spreads her thighs. She's already glistening.

Yeah. It's a good thing no one can see us on this terrace, that no one else gets to see Maisie like this, else I'd have to destroy a few lives. Have to chase them out of the city. And haven't you heard? Hudson Katz has mellowed these days.

For his wife. And only his wife.

No need to get carried away.

* * *

Thanks for reading the Grumps! I hope you loved them. :)

For another crankypants boss, check out Filthy Headlines! *My gorgeous new boss doesn't trust me. Guess I can't blame him. I'm an undercover reporter.*

And for a bonus instalove story, grab your copy of Something Sweet. *I spend every Valentine's Day baking cookies for my friends and neighbors. But the bad boy who just moved to town? He's hungry for something else...*

Happy reading!

xxx

Teaser: Filthy Headlines

❧

Three days later, I step out of the elevator at 8am to a rhythmic pounding floating down the corridor. It's violent, mixed through with pained grunts.

Is Grant Keller... in a fight?

That would make one hell of a story. I drop my bag on my desk and hurry towards his office, my heels sinking into the rug.

"Mr Keller, are you alright?"

His door swings open beneath my palm, and the question dies in my throat.

I've been in here a few times already. Staring around with wide eyes, trying to soak it all in and commit it to memory. And each time, I noticed something new. An artistic sculpture; a high tech gadget. An abstract painting on the wall.

But somehow, I never registered the huge treadmill tucked away in one corner, partly hidden by a screen. It's matte black with sleek lines and sharp corners—the sports car of running equipment.

And sprinting on top of it, elbows pumping and jaw clenched, is Grant Keller.

No: Grant Keller... in a suit.

"Um."

I step further into the office. It's still dark on the street outside, the rows of city windows glowing yellow.

"...Sir?"

His scowl burns into me in the mirror on the far wall. He doesn't even slow down. "What do you want?"

Hmm. What do I want?

I want to know why he's sprinting like wild dogs are chasing him, instead of doing a normal person's workout. I want to know what time he gets here in the mornings. I want to know why he's running in a freaking *suit*. And I kind of want to place my hand between his shoulder blades and feel those muscles flex in his back.

Most of all, though, I want to drag him off that treadmill and push a glass of cold water into his hand. My new 'boss' is wild-eyed, with a light sheen of sweat on his handsome features. His muscles bulge under his suit, so powerful as he runs, but I don't miss the way his hands shake.

What do I want?

I guess right now, I want an answer to my question.

I try again. "Are you alright, sir?"

His scowl deepens. "Is that a personal question, Miss..."

"Jones," I grind out. "Sasha Jones." What an asshole. I've spent the best part of three days in this man's pocket, and he still doesn't know my name?

He must sense my concern dropping away, replaced with cold anger, because he prods a button on the treadmill. The machine slows but doesn't stop, and his sprint turns into a loping walk.

Good. Fine. At least he won't fall on his ass.

"I expect you to knock before you come in here."

"Yes, Mr Keller."

"And there will be no more questions about my well being."

"Noted," I growl.

His mouth twitches in the mirror, like he can sense exactly how much I dislike him. With a deep breath, I smooth my face clear.

Now that he's slowed down, I can look at him without worrying he's about to fall and break his neck. Mr Keller is dressed in a navy suit and pale blue shirt, the collar starched against his throat. He's clean shaven, his body bright with vitality, but his eyes are shadowed.

Interesting.

I shift my weight between my feet, ignoring the flush creeping over my skin. Seeing him being so physical… it does something to me. Makes my stomach flip and my heart race. My traitorous brain can't resist picturing certain things— things like Grant Keller jumping off that treadmill, prowling over here, and crushing me back against the door.

The heat of him.

The smell of his fresh sweat.

Oh god, am I panting?

Pale gray eyes narrow as they watch me closely in the mirror.

"Are you alright, Sasha?"

I lift my chin. Marshal my thoughts. "That sounds like a personal question, Mr Keller."

"I pay you to answer questions."

"No, you pay me to answer phones."

Grant rolls his neck, watching me as he strides along the treadmill. Nerves skitter up my spine.

I can't get fired. If I lose my job here, I'll lose my real job, too.

The one I actually care about.

So I arrange my face into a smile. "Perhaps if you put your question in an email, I'll get to it."

My tone is light, teasing, but he only grunts in reply. Then I scramble out of there like I'm the one being chased by wild dogs.

His office door closes with a snap behind me. I curse Grant Keller under my breath all the way back to my desk, my legs wobbly under my pencil skirt.

It's more than an hour until my cheeks cool.

* * *

Check out Filthy Headlines!

xxx

Cassie Mint

About the Author

Cassie writes outrageous, OTT instalove with tons of sugar and spice. She loves cookie dough, summer barbecues, and her gorgeous cat Missy.

You can connect with me on:

🌐 https://www.authorcassiemint.com

f https://www.facebook.com/cassiemintauthor

🔗 https://www.bookbub.com/authors/cassie-mint

Subscribe to my newsletter:

✉ https://www.authorcassiemint.com/newsletter